Published by:
Powder River Publishing LLC
1014 Black Mountain Road
Thermopolis, Wyoming 82443

Copyright © 2023
ISBN: 978-1-956881-04-2
Cover design: Ryan Collins
Printed in the United States of America

www.powderriverpublishing.com

THIS BOOK IS DEDICATED TO THE INDIGENOUS PEOPLE
OF THE WORLD WHO ENDURED MUCH AND CONTINUE TO
ENDURE.

Citations

Page 18*: McLaughlin, James. My Friend the Indian
(Expanded, Annotated) (pp. 7-10). BIG BYTE BOOKS.
Kindle Edition.

Page 28*: McLaughlin, James. My Friend the Indian (Expanded, Annotated) (p. 133-143). BIG BYTE
BOOKS. Kindle Edition.

Page 48*: McLaughlin, James. My Friend the Indian (Expanded, Annotated) (p. 144-164). BIG BYTE
BOOKS. Kindle Edition.

Page 58*: Wyoming State Archives and Historical
Department (p.7-14).

Contents

Introduction

The Wind River becomes the Big Horn River at a shallow stretch of water now called the "Wedding of the Waters." This is where this story began.

The river makes its way from rocky snow-capped peaks in the nearby Wind River Mountains.

It flows unaturally wild, moving north through Wyoming and Montana on its way to meet up with the Columbia River and then eventually the Mississippi before it empties out into the Gulf of Mexico.

The River itself is a testement to time and determination. It has cut its way through rock and millenia, crumbling a path through the Wind River Canyon to a grand opening that leads to the Basin.

The Wind River and the Big Horn River is the same river with two different names. It was given those names by two different peoples, who had different views on the changing world they lived in.

The river still has two different names and the Wedding of the Waters is still the border between two different worlds.

Manifest Destiny

April 19, 1893

In the days of the first man, they came upon this place. They came upon it, drawn to the smoking waters they believed held the spirits themselves.

The waters are a sacred place of the spirits.

Those first days when the water was found by man were looked upon as a gift from the gods themselves. The heat of the water warmed from the center of the earth has always been good medicine for men. They heal every ailment that afflicts the human body and spirit.

Our people have used the waters long after the days of these first men. Our time here now is drawing to an end. The settlers come onto our land in greater and greater numbers and use the waters however they see fit. It is no longer the sacred place we held for ourselves.

Our game is leaving us.

We tell a story of how our people found the waters.

A beautiful chiefess and her warrior chief got lost in the great canyon of the Wind River, eventually finding a way when the feather she held in her hair was carried away by the wind.

They followed the feather blowing in the wind until it landed in the smoking waters.

Gazing upon these ancient waters, they felt as these first men felt, that they were in a sacred place where the spirits meet the earth.

The animals once roamed here, numerous and plentiful. But now they are no longer here. A distant memory of a different time. Now my people are turning to a different way of life.

My chief and father has always been a friend to the Great Father in Washington. He has never met the man.

"Why do you tell me these things? There is nothing I can do to help you now. The only thing to do now is to sell it to the great father and get as much as you can before your father dies."

"You know that he doesn't want to leave, but now I think he is ready, Inspector.

The great chief Washakie.

You have been here before, you know what it is like."

"This time is different, and this time I come with more money. You must help me make your father realize the time has come and there will never be a better offer than now."

"Do you see the way this river flows, Agent McLaughlin?"

"Yes, I see it. It flows north."

"It flows like the spirit of our people, against the very nature of things. It will not be easy to get him to agree with you and your money. It will be even harder to get the Shoshone and Arapahoe to agree on anything together. They are sworn enemies."

"Please talk with your father, Dick. I will be back by the spring moon with the offer from the Great Father and Washington. It will be the last time they try to buy this place and if the offer is refused, there will be no money for your father. I know he wants to enjoy the fruits of his labor before he goes with those great spirits that have come before him and he has known, but he will have to get Sharp Nose to accept the offer with him as Washington will make one offer to both the tribes. I know this burden is much for you to handle, but this is why I talk with you now in secret. I trust you and your judgment."

"You have been good to our people agent McLaughlin. You are known to us and have been fair to us. You have our trust and respect, but you know the chiefs. They will want this deal to be fair as they will be giving a sacred place to a government that has taken much. If the deal is not straight and fair, there will be no deal. You must assure the chiefs the government will not steal from our people or be dishonest."

"Dick, you bear the great name of Washakie and you do your people proud. These are changing times, the West is evaporating and will soon be tamed. The things we have known will soon be a distant memory of the past. You and I have both seen things change in our own time. Right now is the time to get what retributions you can for your people, and for the Aprapahoe. You and I both know that the government wants to develop these lands. Utah will become a state soon, and these territories will follow soon thereafter. Cleveland will no longer be the Great Father soon and I fear our country is taking a different aim, one that you and I have seen before."

"We have seen this before, James."

"I do this for the love of your people and the land. I will do all I can do to ensure everything is fair and the word is upheld. We have come far you and I. You have shown me the beauty of this land, and for that, I am indebted to you, Dick."

"I will speak with my father, and you speak with your people in Washington. Make sure that they give our people what we deserve for these sacred lands, James.

There is no price for land and no claim to the sacred lands of the spirits. You cannot own these lands, James and your people will come to understand that in time.

We must allow the people, and our people to have free access to these waters where the first men discovered the spirits of the earth."

"The great wind always changes, moving us and our people to our destiny. This place is of both our people and our future, which is intertwined now for better or for worse."

Tomorrow is not Yesterday

Three years later…

"Mr. Vice President, we have a letter for you from Indian Agent, James McLaughlin. It's regarding the reservation land with the hot springs in Wyoming, near Yellowstone."

"Oh give it to me already. Not only do we face the end of our glorious run, but we face this new way that has come along with the political winds."

"Here you are sir, as presented. May this new way remember you and Mr. Cleveland's great successes as they truly have been."

"Nothing is remembered as it was, only remembered the way we want to. There's a collective mindset with this sort of thing, I've come to find.

Now then, what does our esteemed Indian Agent have to say on the matter?"

"It would seem, sir, Mr. McLaughlin has procured an arrangement to purchase a plot of land totaling 10 square miles from the Shoshone and Arapahoe for a price of $60,000. These monies are to be paid to the tribes in yearly installments, the first of which is to be in cash. The rest is to be paid in yearly installments of goods. Mostly coffee and beef from what I can deduce, sir."

Adlai Ewing Stevenson, the Vice President of the United States of America took a moment to examine the paperwork, growing tired of the minute details involved. Numbers and logistics rattled around in his head like a caged songbird.

McLaughlin. Wasn't that the man who ordered Sitting Bull's arrest?

"How much do the Indians want, and why does our man McLaughlin believe these lands are valuable to the United States government? Enough with the introduction, give it to me then. What does he think?"

"Sir, I have the honor to transmit herewithin an agreement made and concluded April 21, 1896, by and between James McLaughlin, United States Indian Inspector, on part of the United States, and the Shoshone and Arapahoe tribes of Indians, in the state of Wyoming, whereby the Indians cede to the United States a portion of their reservation, embracing the Owl Creek and Big Horn Springs."

The Vice President took a moment to absorb the agreement.

'What does McLaughlin write of his experience? I know he's been poking around over there near where Custer met his wretched fate. I say nothing good is going to come from this thirst for expansion. Rome met its end the same way. We have no business rounding these people up and stealing their land, but nobody listens to that sort of rhetoric. Everyone wants something to be done, with no thought of the consequences."

"As the acting Assistant Secretary of the State, sir, and as a former Confederate soldier, I urge you to consider the words that our agent has written to us of his service. Custer may have won the Civil War for the union, but he lost the battle for the nation's soul."

"Thank you for that Sims. I would prefer to hear it from the agent after all. He, unlike yourself, took his cause upon himself and went out West to see what it was like for himself."

"Very well, sir, here it is:

"I arrived at Shoshone Agency on the evening of the 4th instant, after a journey of 150 miles by stage over wretchedly bad roads at this season of the year from Rawlins, Wyo., having been three days in making the trip. On Wednesday the 8th instant, I left the agency, accompanied by three Shoshone and three Arapahoe Indians, two interpreters — one from each tribe and Mr. John Small, agency miller, to visit the Big Horn Hot Springs, situated on the northeastern corner of the Shoshone Reservation, about 70 miles distant from the agency, by the trail which crosses the Owl Creek range of mountains through what is known as the Red Canyon route. We returned by another trail, following up Owl Creek 38 miles, crossed the Owl Creek Mountains at that point, and thence the agency, traveling a distance of 100 miles on our return trip. I returned by this route at the request of the Indians to look over the northern portion of their reservation, so that I might see if the whites who occupy the adjacent country, were trespassing upon the timber of their reservation. Capt. R. H. Wilson, acting Indian agent, furnished me with transportation for the journey, and we were seven days in making the round trip.

I examined the springs and country surrounding them very carefully, and while I found the country very rough and broken, with numerous high buttes and deep gulches, yet the northern slopes are well sodded and furnish very fair grazing for cattle or sheep, and in the tract of 10 miles up the Big Horn River, from the mouth of Owl Creek, and 10 miles wide, secured by the cession as per the inclosed agreement, there is about 1,000 acres of good ariable bottom land. The Big Wind River, which has its source in the Rocky Mountains and which runs through the Shoshone Reservation trending northeast, after passing through the canyon of the Owl Mountains, is known as the Big Horn River. The canyon is cut of solid rock through the Owl Mountains several hundred feet deep. It is about 9 miles long, with almost perpendicular rock walls. The Hot Springs are up the Big Horn River about 4 miles from the mouth of Owl Creek, and about 6 miles from the mouth of said canyon, which is about 2 miles from the southeastern corner of the ceded 10-mile tract.

The main or principal spring is on the east side of the Big Horn River, and the mountain scenery at this point is magnificent. This spring is truly wonderful: the surface is about 30 feet across, circular in form, a seething boiling cauldron, with a temperature of 132° degrees fahrenheit., and discharging a volume of water estimated at 1,250,000 gallons every twenty-four hours. The water of this spring is said to possess wonderful curative properties and to be very beneficial for rheumatic and other ailments, and although the temperature is 132° it is not unpleasant to drink, and that with salt and pepper added tastes very much like fresh chicken broth. The analysis of the water of this spring by Professor Schutzenburger, or the College of France, member of the institute and Academy at the instance of his friend, Dr. J. A. Scheulke, of Lander, Wyoming is as follows."

"The good Doctor goes on to name the specific properties found in the water, Mr. Vice President. Do you want to hear the analysis, sir?"

"That won't be necessary, Sims. I assume that the land is mineral rich. Am I correct in that assumption?"

"You are indeed, Mr. Vice President. McLaughlin continues on in his writing of his experience. Would you like me to continue on, sir?"

"Please, man. Do continue."

"Very well, sir, here it is:

There are numerous other springs in the neighborhood, also in the bed of the Big Horn River, adjacent to the main spring, which is continually bubbling in the channel of lava formation, apparently extinct springs or geysers, and in the immediate vicinity of the springs there is a mountain of crystallized gypsum.

I was instructed not to pay the Indians exceeding $50,000 for the springs and the tract of land embracing them, especially for a 5 by 10-mile tract, and that if negotiations were conducted on a basis of a certain price per acre, I should in no event agree to pay to exceed $1.25 per acre. After an examination of the springs and the adjacent country, and ascertaining from the course of Owl Creek, which trends slightly to the northeast, that a tract 10 miles long on the eastern boundary and 10 miles wide on the southern boundary, and from the southwestern corner due north to Owl Creek, would give about 86 sections of land (55,040 acres), only just and reasonable for the tract ceded, including the said springs, and I concluded the agreement with the Indians for said amount.

The Indians of this reservation are receiving only a ration of beef and flour and are not sufficiently provided with food, and as they are now making commendable efforts in farming, I concluded, after consulting with the acting Indian Agent and others familiar with their condition, that a small ration of bacon, coffee, and sugar, for a period of five years would be most beneficial in aiding them in their agricultural efforts, and from the progress they are now making, and the excellent country they occupy, they
should, in five years, be well advanced in agriculture and on the road to providing for their family wants through their own industry.

The census shows 457 males over 18 years of age belonging on the reservation, 180 Shoshones, and 93 Arapahoes, a total of 273. All who were present at the agency signed the agreement. Others arrived from distant parts of the reservation after the rolls were closed and certificates made, and as I had 44 more than half of the Indians qualified to sign, I did not deem it necessary to reopen the rolls which would have necessitated changing the certificates. There was not a single Indian who refused to sign or offered any objections after the agreement was reached.

The agreement was the best that I could make, and consider it just to the United States and to the Indians, and trust that It will meet with your approval and early ratification by Congress.

I enclose (sic) herewith minutes of the proceedings of the several councils held with the Indians regarding the cession of the springs.

l am, sir, very respectfully, your obedient servant, signed James McLaughlin, United States Indian Inspector."

The Vice President pondered these new lands in his head, envisioning the place he had never been. The very thought of McLaughlin traversing these lands, seeing things he may never see made him untrusting of the situation.

"I cannot make a determination on the matter until I hear it from the horse's mouth. Bring me, Colonel McLaughlin. I want to hear from his own lips what it is we are getting ourselves into. He seems to have a certain fondness for these people and I want to know why."

"Very well sir, we will send for him this instant," the Assistant Secretary of State answered.

If I Had It My Way

Morning droplets slid from fresh green foliage, eclipsing through rainbow in the rising May sun. Smoke whimpered haphazardly from the campfire, mostly solitary coals breathing in the slight breeze.

Hooves broke through the moistened soil, thundering through half-dead sagebrush, twisted and thirsty in an endless pursuit of nonexistent water.

A rider arrived at the threshold of the fort and dismounted. He approached the commanding officer, who was Captain John S. Loud.

Not even the morning could wait for the message bound to Colonel James McLaughlin, who lay warm in his camp on the edge of Fort Washakie.

"There is a message for the Inspector Colonel. It's from Washington."

"Where did you ride from, Sargeant?"

"Sir?" the rider answered the man, staring at his stripes which outranked him.

"Where did you ride from to deliver this message from Sargeant?" Captain Loud asked again.

The rider caught his breath and answered, "From Cheyenne, Captain."

"How was your ride?"

The Sargeant reflected on his tumultuous journey, shifting his stance. His tailbone still had a dull continuous throbbing.

"There wasn't much trouble, sir. The road was

difficult at times, but that's to be expected."

"What is the nature of this message from Washington that required of you to make the sojourn from Cheyenne, Sargeant?"

"I mean no disrespect to a man of your rank, but the message is intended for Inspector McLaughlin's eyes only."

"It's a secret message then?"

"A message from Washington, Captain."

"Very well, I will inform the Colonel Inspector of the message you carry from Washington."

Loud left the sergeant and walked in the direction of McLaughlin's tent. He didn't envy McLaughlin's duties but tried to understand them.

"Inspector, sorry to wake you so early, but there is a rider from Washington carrying a message. He has said the message is for your personage only."

McLaughlin, the Indian Agent stepped out of his tent, fashioned in the native american tradition of te-pees. He liked the convenience and ruggedness the te-pees offered in the conditions the West presented. He was already dressed. He could not sleep the night before.

McLaughlin looked out on the May morning and the waiting rider, carrying his coming fate.

"And how has the morning found you, Captain?" asked McLaughlin of his fellow officer.

"Like most mornings out here, James, cold and without the prospect of swimming in the ocean anytime soon."

The two men walked together, dressed in their uniforms that gave testament to their employer. Their buttons shined with the effort given forth by the two. Every detail was taken to account and addressed with conscious.

As they approached the trail-weary Sargeant, he looked upon them with a steadfast look of duty, his mission within reach of accomplishment.

"Sargeant," McLaughlin said to the man. "Let's have these orders from Washington and see what they will have of me this time."

The Sargeant quickly produced the articles he was tasked with delivering to McLaughlin.

The Sargeant and Lieutenant watched as McLaughlin read over the orders from Washington.

Inspector,

The Vice President is unsure of the report you submitted and requires an explanation in person. He wants to hear it from you yourself James.

Humbly, WM. H. Simms

Assistant Secretary of the Interior

"Sargeant, have my men tend to your horse and get yourself something to eat. You have a long ride back and so do we in the coming days."

"Thank you, sir," he said, looking at the man who ordered the arrest of Sitting Bull as he left them and went about his life.

"What is it, James? What do they want from you?"

"John, they want me to come back to Washington and explain the report. What it sounds like is they are unsure of what to do and need more advice beyond what is found in the report."

"You made a fair deal James. A fair deal on both sides that will stand the test of time."

"History doesn't remember the one who made the deal, it remembers those that live through the deal. This deal has no more of a chance of standing the test of time than any of the other treaties made on behalf of the government with the natives. There has to be a will to be just and fair, That will has wavered, or maybe it was never there in the first place," McLaughlin said, looking out at Fort Washakie.

"You gave them the report and told them everything there was to tell about the deal. Either they want to make it happen, or they don't. What difference will it make to bring you to Washington and explain to them what is in the report?"

"It's more than that, John. They want to see me, the man who has tamed the West of the Indian problem. They want to see the man who has made some of their troubles go away at a reasonably cheap price."

"Washakie, his son and all the others will remember what you have done, James." The Captain looked out at the vastness of plains surrounding them and the fort that offered sanctuary amongst the wild untamed land. It was his duty to protect those who lived within the fort and he saw it as McLaughlin's duty to protect those who lived outside the fort and those who would one day live there.

"This business is almost done. I wish we could have given them more for the land, but I gave them the most I could. More than I was told I could give them. They are close to making their farms work, but I fear the land is too harsh to make anything come from it and the way of life is worlds from the lives they once knew. It will be hard for them to make it work and I hope this sale will give them what they need to make that way of life happen. There will be other deals to make after this and it will be my duty to make sure that they get a fair chance at making it. Those chiefs are near their end, it will be their sons and daughter that inherit the mess that will be left to them and it will be up to them to make it work in the new world that has been left for them."

The Captain pondered on this for a moment before asking, "What do you think will become of the place itself?

"What do you mean, John?"

"What do you think the government will do with the waters?"

"I hope they will make it a place of healing for everyone who seeks it. I hope they make it a place where the healing will happen someday."

"Do you think that will ever happen, James?"

"Not in our lifetime, but one day this will be a place where people come from around the world to seek the healing waters. It's already been like that to this point in history and I see it has the potential to be world-renowned. Its location does it no favors, but I think that adds to the allure of the place. It makes it more sacred."

"What would you have given them for the waters, James? If you could have had it your way of course."

"I would have given them the buffalo back."

The two men smiled on this point and went about their morning, talking about the fort and the men garrisoned within it.

Loud made arrangements to prepare McLaughlin for his journey back to Cheyenne, where he would catch a train from the edge of civilization to the heart of the nation where decisions blew like tumbleweeds from east to west.

The Ghost Dance

Mclaughlin watched the world through his lonely window. He was heading directly into the civilized world he had tried to escape. And yet here he was, traveling to the city to explain the wonders of the frontier and the natives to men who could not understand either. Memories filled his mind of the losses and pains he had endured through his employment for the federal government.

He was a new man now. A man free of the things that haunted his soul, now able to move unhindered by the weight of the burden that had pushed down on him for so long. It had taken some time to get free of the expectations he held as novelties, probably derived from boyhood tales of romance and adventure. He had found the adventure his youthful self had yearned for.

He came to learn that adventure is not always a boyhood fairy tale and it often leads to unspeakable tragedy that coarsely rubs the soul raw.

These were the things inaccurately described in the dime novels of his youth. He knew now the authors had not lived those experiences themselves. They were mere fantasies and he had bought in, only to learn the reality of humanity.

Love. A word that now brought many feelings and thoughts to his mind. What was it to love? Was it giving every part of yourself and your soul until there is nothing left to give? He wasn't sure anymore, all he was sure of was the land. That was love to McLaughlin. There was nothing more than the sweet mother that moved in perpetuated freedom throughout the seasons across the great expanses of the West. He had come to know it intimately.

He held the smells and sounds in reverence and thanked the lord he was able to experience such sweet joy in his soul. He longed for the land and feared for what it might become. The kind of fear one holds because they have felt the throngs of loss and know it intimately.

It had taken some time for him to begin to see the land. It came through in waves he could barely understand, but over time the land made its way through him. He began to understand it and respect it. It made him see things differently. He saw the way they lived with the land. It was in unison with the earth, not in domination of it.

He saw their connection with the animals of the land and it made him feel as though they understood they were a part of something bigger than themselves. It all made sense to him and it gave him hope for humanity, that maybe there had been a great understanding reached at some point, but now it was just forgotten. It could be reached again one day if man just returned to the land. It made him think of the days he was a boy in Ontario. Life was different back then.

He would play in his neighborhood with the other boys, dreaming of a future full of adventure and hope. They would play war, and he never understood the point.

What would he tell the Vice President, or better yet, what would that boyhood version of himself say? Would he tell it like it is? Tell them all the things he had seen from his eyes, or tell them the truth from their eyes?

He knew the fate of the Arapahoe and Shoshone were at hand. He did not want to be responsible for the destruction of their storied tribe. His soul could not handle another Sitting Bull.

He remembered the day Sitting Bull died while the train carried him through the land on its way to Washington D.C. and the heart of the nation which consumes other nations and men entirely. His own heartfelt consumed by the memory of what happened. It was the classic tale of survival of the fittest, working itself out in human history as the great American West faded into the memory of those who had the chance to see it before it got overrun.

One day he would put it all down in writing. He would try explaining these misunderstood people he had lived with and seeing their way of life.

"Their way of life will be nothing more than a memory if it is not written down and explained from the outside objective perspective," McLaughlin often told others when asked about his experiences.

He often struggled to put into words the things he had seen and experienced living amongst the plain Indians. He knew it would be even harder to one day sit down and collect his thoughts and put it all down in writing the best he could, all these things he had bore witness to. He knew it was a duty to tell the world what he knew, but for now, there was more work to be done.

"Lord, let me learn from the mistakes of my past," he would say at the end of his prayer every night. "Forgive me for my sins and for playing the role I did in the loss of such a great man, my friend the Indian."

McLaughlin pulled out his notebook after he could no longer stand to see the land he loved so much fade further and further away. He began to write.

*"In the later sixties (1860s) an impossible condition had arisen in the relations of the white man and the Indian. The Caucasian had wheeled the car of progress up to the border of the Indian land and had been compelled to halt until the red man had been coerced, cajoled, or compelled to get out of the way. Coercion and cajolery had been pretty well worn out on the Indian, and he had come to some sort of knowledge of the fact that he must make a stand. During the Civil War, and in the unsettled period succeeding it, he had broken loose from the leading-strings of the agents and had things pretty much his own way. His roaming had not been materially interfered with, and there is no doubt that he felt very well able to take care of himself without any guidance from the white man. The care that had been bestowed upon him when he consented, theretofore, to render himself amenable to the arguments offered—backed by fleshpots—by the whites, was not just what would appeal to any man, white or red. There had been a good deal of chicanery in the administration of Indian affairs. He had been starved into rebellion and beaten—sometimes—into submission. But during the war he had tasted again the delights of practically unhampered freedom. That this freedom took the form of horrid license at times was shown by the awful outbreaks indulged in on the frontiers. Those of the Indians who lived in countries which were not yet desired by the whites were living a wild, free life in the midst of what they regarded as plenty. There is no doubt that the roving bands were a menace to travel on the plains, and that they would

have to be put on reservations if the white man was to be permitted to carry out the great promise of which the time was pregnant.

The entire regular army—or practically all of it—was afield in pursuit of the Indians. General Sheridan, whose opinion of the people he was engaged in checking or fighting was summed in the phrase, "There are no good Indians but dead Indians," was in command in the field on the frontier. General Sherman, whose notion of dealing with the Indian was expressed in the statement that they must be suppressed by "merciless and vindictive warfare," was at the head of the army. These same sentiments, as regarded the whites, were evidently held to by the chiefs of the fierce and warlike tribes of Teton Sioux, the Cheyennes, Comanches, Kiowas, Apaches, and others, whose business was the chase primarily, but plunder and war when ill-treatment gave excuse for reprisals. In view of the expressed sentiments of the great military leaders of the times, the attitude of the Indian is not calculated to cause great surprise—viewed now at a distance of thirty-five or forty years. At the time of the accession of General Grant to the presidency every man's hand was raised against the Indian, and, it must be admitted, the Indian had his hand raised against white men generally. I do not mean that all the Indians were inclined to the warpath, but the greater portion of the warlike tribes were afield and ready for trouble.

And they were a very different body of men, physically, from the Indians of today. They wore an air of sturdy independence. They were equipped according to their natural requirements. Their minds were generally attuned to magnificent ideas of time and distance. They abhorred the limitations that the white man accepts as affecting his dwelling-place. They were foes to be reckoned with, or they might be converted into friends worth the having. It is a matter for profound regret that the Indian of that day could not have been advanced to his present knowledge of, and capacity for, civilized pursuits without being subjected to the debasing and degenerating physical and moral conditions that were inseparable from the processes of transmutation.

Just previous to the inauguration of General Grant, commissions, composed largely of military men, had proposed treaties to the more important of the tribes. They had accepted the treaties, or some of their chiefs had; and when General Grant, in his inaugural, proclaimed the peace policy in dealing with the Indian, there was a fair prospect that the shedding of blood on the frontier would cease. And it might have ceased if the Indian could have been protected from his fool friends in authority, and the white man freed in the smallest degree from the promptings of cupidity that would tolerate no delay in grasping the riches that had been the portion of the red man. From the time of the signing of the treaties of 1868 up to the date of my entrance into the Indian service, in 1871, there had been very large accessions to the number of Indians living at the agencies. On the extreme frontier there had been fighting, and many isolated but bloody encounters took place. But the Indian was different from what he had been a few years previously. In the language of the bounding West in which he made his habitat, it may be said that, in 1871, the Indian was "halter-broke but he had not yet been bitted." That was to come later, when the bloody arbitrament of war had been appealed to and the mighty tide of white men had engulfed and submerged the red bands that stood in the way to the setting sun and fortune. The operation of the law of the survival of the fittest has not been applied, according to the Indian canons of fitness, and the great men of the red race, the last of a race of physical giants, have passed away in the years that have intervened since 1871. They have not yet been succeeded by the race of mental giants that should follow them. But in the process of eliminating the big men of the race, some stirring events took place. In some of these events I had a part, of many I was an interested observer. And the relation of these events will properly include the story of the passing of the Indian of yesterday.

Born in 1842, in the province of Ontario, of Irish and Scotch ancestry,—an accident of birth the distinction of which I gladly share with some millions of my contemporaries,—I arrived in Minnesota in 1863, with two strong, bare hands, and entered into an apprenticeship for a career among the Indians by becoming acquainted with many of them and of their mixed bloods at St. Paul, Mendota, Wabasha, Faribault, and other places in that then frontier state. I had acquired some slight knowledge of the Sioux language, and when, in 1871, Major W. H. Forbes was appointed agent at Devils Lake agency, in what is now North Dakota, and offered me a place, with virtual charge of the outfit he was taking into the Sioux country, I was in some measure equipped for the position by an understanding of the manners and customs of the Sioux. Looking back down the vista of years, I see now that I was not nearly so well equipped for a life among the Indians as I thought I was when I mounted a horse and navigated a bull- train of twenty yoke of cattle and ten wagons out through the streets of St. Paul in the early morning of July 1, 1871."*

He stopped writing and looked out the window. The west in question had now long faded into the planes of the midwest. Looking around at the other military passengers on the train, he considered what they would really want to hear. He had seen so many changes in administrations and political ideology that he had forgotten who was in charge now and who was just elected. They would want to hear about the deal itself, not the Indian problem.

They would want to hear the dollar and cents of it all and how to avoid further conflict. They wanted to hear how I came to terms for this deal in order to replicate it and weaponize it. There was no explaining the gift of the waters without explaining the past, or at least some of it. The writing helped him makes sense of it all in his mind when it all seemed a jumbled mess of broken dreams and lives.

He looked outside his window again, then closed his eyes. He imagined looking at Sitting Bull for the last time, then he began to write.

WHEN SITTING BULL'S MEDICINE FAILED

*"I stood by the grave of Sitting Bull one Sunday evening a few months ago. The mound under which is buried the body of the medicine man is in the extreme northwest corner of the Fort Yates military cemetery, adjoining the Standing Rock Agency, North Dakota. It is marked with the stenciled inscription, in black on a white board:—
SITTING BULL
DIED
December 15, 1890.

There was no other grave within thirty yards. A profound peace lay upon the place. Far up toward the agency school a number of Indian boys played croquet; a phonograph in the Indian police-headquarters was working,— working,—as it is most of the time,—and oddly enough it was reproducing "Taps" from a bugler's record. Two hundred yards east of the grave of Sitting Bull the deserted barracks of Fort Yates afforded a dismal playground for the children of the agency employees, and their voices came faintly down to the cemetery; in the northwest the sun was dropping out of sight behind the buttes. A more lovely landscape, a scene more replete with the suggestion of a holy peace, could not be imagined; and there at my feet lay, stilled forever, the form which had been the tenement of the turbulent spirit of Sitting Bull, who had striven all his life to bar the progress of the white man, who made the setting for this all-pervading peace, while a few rods away stood the dismantled fort built to hold that spirit in check. The deserted fort and the dead hostile spoke to me of the passing of the day of the Indian, and as the peal of the vesper bell floated down from the mission chapel on the hill, I was minded to tell the story of the death of Sitting Bull.

Crafty, avaricious, mendacious, and ambitious, Sitting Bull possessed all of the faults of an Indian and none of the nobler attributes which have gone far to redeem some of his people from their deeds of guilt. He had no single quality that would serve to draw his people to him, yet he was by far the most influential man of his nation for many years,—neither Gall, Spotted Tail, nor Red Cloud, all greater men in every sense, exerting the power he did. I never knew him to display a single trait that might command admiration or respect, and I knew him well in the later years of his life. But he maintained his prestige by the acuteness of his mind and his knowledge of human nature. Even his people knew him as a physical coward, but the fact did not handicap the man in dealing with his following. He had many defenders at all times, and his medicine was good down to the end.

He was not a hereditary chief, nor even a chief by election or choice. He was born in 1834 on the Grand River, South Dakota, within twenty miles of the scene of his death. His father's name was Sitting Bull, and the son was called, as a boy, Jumping Badger. I had his history from his own lips when he returned, in May, 1883, from his imprisonment at Fort Randall, where he was held after his surrender in 1881. He got his name and made his first entrance into the public life of his band—the Hunkpapa—by the use of that intelligence which he displayed through life.

As a boy of fourteen, he told me,—and the facts were well known to the people,—that he accompanied his father and their tribesmen on one occasion when the Sioux took the war-path against the Crows. In a battle a Crow warrior was killed. Jumping Badger did not kill the man, but he counted the coup,—touched the body first after death,—and established his right to be regarded as the slayer. Upon the return of this war-party to the village, Jumping Badger's father made a feast, gave away a great many ponies, and announced that his son had won the right to wear his father's name and should thenceforth be known as Sitting Bull—in which the old man made provision beyond his knowing for the perpetuation of the name. His accuracy of judgment, knowledge of men, a student-like disposition to observe natural phenomena, and a deep insight into affairs among Indians and such white people as he came into contact with, made his stock in trade, and he made "good medicine." He made a pretence at mysticism that was easily sustained among his people, and long before the Custer affair he had a high standing among the common people and was too high to be injured by the contempt of the war-chiefs.

There is no doubt that his medicine was good in the Custer affair. He foretold with great accuracy the battle and the event, and the mere fact that he took to the hills, there to make medicine, while the fight was in progress, did not affect his standing adversely. He came out of the affair with higher honor than he possessed when he went into it. The disastrous retreat to Canada, and the sufferings his people underwent while he was leading them, caused him a considerable loss in prestige. Gall and Crow King, his chief lieutenants, found him to be a fraud and a coward, and deserted him. Hump of the Minniconjou left him and surrendered. Rain-in-the-Face and other hereditary chiefs of his people despised him as an incompetent leader and coward, and brought their people in. Sitting Bull surrendered at Fort Buford in July, 1881, and when I first came in contact with him personally he was a prisoner. Officially I had been watching him for years.

It was on the day I arrived to take charge of the agency at Standing Rock, September 8, 1881, that I saw him first. He was a prisoner on board the steamer General Sherman. The boat had brought me down from Bismarck, and was ordered to take on board at Fort Yates, near the agency, Sitting Bull and one hundred and forty-six of his fellow prisoners, for transport to Fort Randall. Sitting Bull and his people were on board when I went down to the steamer after getting my things ashore. He had sent for me to tell me of his grievances. He was a stocky man, with an evil face and shifty eyes, and he still showed the effect of his desperate experience of five years in the Canadian Northwest, chiefly in the Province of Alberta. He knew of me, and what little he said was without his usual arrogance, for he was then desirous of making friends. I saw no more of him until he was released as a prisoner of war and sent from Fort Randall, Dakota Territory, and came under my jurisdiction at Standing Rock on May 10, 1883 where he lived up to the time of his death, and where I succeeded in keeping him out of mischief generally until 1890.

KICKING BEAR AND THE COMING OF THE GHOSTS

It was in the early fall of 1890 that Kicking Bear, a half-crazed fanatic of the Minniconjou band, came up from the Cheyenne River reservation and imparted to Sitting Bull the secrets of the new religion which would bring the Indian into the inheritance of the earth. As an exhorter Kicking Bear was a power, but he had no force as a leader. The doctrine he came to spread was contrived with such ingenuity that it is still a wonder to me that it did not spread further among a people so much given to superstitions that accepted spiritism as the foundation of all things religious. It took a tremendous hold upon those who became at all infected with the new belief.

There has been much speculation as to the origin of the Messianic movement. The Indians said it came from a people "who lived beyond the Yellow Faces to the west of the Utes." This led me to believe that the craze took form at the instigation of some genius of the southwestern tribes, who had observed the practices of those descendants of the Aztecs who look to the east every morning in anticipation of the return of Montezuma, who is to redeem them from toil and subjection and set them to rule over the earth. The new belief had traveled far in a brief space of time, and sprang into vigorous life almost in a day on the Standing Rock reservation. It looked like an inspired outbreak of religious zeal. As a matter of fact I am convinced that the new religion was managed from the beginning, so far as the Standing Rock Sioux were concerned, by Sitting Bull, who had heard of the new faith that was making some headway in the southern reservations, and who, having lost his former influence over the Sioux, planned to import and use it to reestablish himself in the leadership of the people, whom he might then lead in safety in any desperate enterprise which he might direct.

During the summer of that year I was repeatedly compelled to refuse Sitting Bull permission to visit the Cheyenne River reservation. Some reports had come to us of the introduction of the "Ghost-Dancing" religion in the southern reservations, and I declined to allow Sitting Bull to leave his home. He had established himself with his family and friends on the Grand River, forty miles southwest of the agency, and was under the espionage of Indians upon whose fidelity I could reckon; and that dependence was warranted even to the death, it was shown.

Sitting Bull had heard of Kicking Bear. That individual had been absent from home for about a year, and had begun to preach the new religion on his return. Finding that he could not get away himself, Sitting Bull sent six of his young men to Cherry Creek, on the Cheyenne River reservation, with an invitation to Kicking Bear to make him, Sitting Bull, a visit. The Minniconjou medicine man arrived at Grand River October 9, 1890, and forthwith initiated Sitting Bull into the mysteries of the new cult. I had never seen Kicking Bear at that time, but had learned of the doctrine upon which he based his preaching, the "revelation," from the lips of One Bull, a nephew of Sitting Bull, who repeated to me word for word, with that accuracy of memory that marks the unlettered, the preachment of Kicking Bear. One Bull, an Indian policeman at the time, imparted what he had heard of the new dispensation with obvious trepidation, but with some sense of security, because he had found that Sitting Bull's medicine was no longer good. I set the matter down at the time in the words of Kicking Bear, as repeated by One Bull, and here it is:—

"My brothers, I bring to you the promise of a day in which there will be no white man to lay his hand on the bridle of the Indian's horse; when the red men of the prairie will rule the world and not be turned from the hunting-grounds by any man. I bring you word from your fathers the ghosts, that they are now marching to join you, led by the Messiah who came once to live on earth with the white men, but was cast out and killed by them. I have seen the wonders of the spirit-land, and have talked with the ghosts. I traveled far and am sent back with a message to tell you to make ready for the coming of the Messiah and return of the ghosts in the spring.

"In my tepee on the Cheyenne reservation I arose

after the corn-planting, sixteen moons ago, and prepared for my journey. I had seen many things and had been told by a voice to go forth and meet the ghosts, for they were to return and inhabit the earth. I traveled far on the cars of the white men, until I came to the place where the railroad stopped. There I met two men, Indians, whom I had never seen before, but who greeted me as a brother and gave me meat and bread. They had three horses, and we rode without talking for four days, for I knew they were to be witnesses to what I should see. Two suns had we traveled, and had passed the last signs of the white man,—for no white man had ever had the courage to travel so far,—when we saw a strange and fierce- looking black man, dressed in skins. He was living alone, and had medicine with which he could do what he wished. He would wave his hands and make great heaps of money; another motion, and we saw many spring wagons, already painted and ready to hitch horses to; yet another motion of the hands, and there sprung up before us great herds of buffalo. The black man spoke and told us that he was the friend of the Indian; that we should remain with him and go no farther, and we might take what we wanted of the money, and spring wagons, and the buffalo. But our hearts were turned away from the black man, my brothers, and we left him and traveled for two days more.

"On the evening of the fourth day, when we were weak and faint from our journey, we looked for a camping-place, and were met by a man dressed like an Indian, but whose hair was long and glistening like the yellow money of the white man. His face was very beautiful to see, and when he spoke my heart was glad and I forgot my hunger and the toil I had gone through.

And he said, 'How, my children. You have done well to make this long journey to come to me. Leave your horses and follow me.' And our hearts sang in our breasts and we were glad. He led the way up a great ladder of small clouds, and we followed him up through an opening in the sky. My brothers, the tongue of Kicking Bear is straight and he cannot tell all that he saw, for he is not an orator, but the forerunner and herald of the ghosts. He whom we followed took us to the Great Spirit and his wife, and we lay prostrate on the ground, but I saw that they were dressed as Indians. Then from an opening in the sky we were shown all the countries of the earth and the camping-grounds of our fathers since the beginning; all were there, the tepees, and the ghosts of our fathers, and great herds of buffalo, and a country that smiled because it was rich and the white man was not there. Then he whom we had followed showed us his hands and feet, and there were wounds in them which had been made by the whites when he went to them and they crucified him. And he told us that he was going to come again on earth, and this time he would remain and live with the Indians, who were his chosen people.

"Then we were seated on rich skins, of animals unknown to me, before the open door of the tepee of the Great Spirit, and told how to say the prayers and perform the dances I am now come to show my brothers. And the Great Spirit spoke to us saying:—
"'Take this message to my red children and tell it to them as I say it. I have neglected the Indians for many moons, but I will make them my people now if they obey me in this message. The earth is getting old, and I will make it new for my chosen people, the Indians, who are to inhabit it, and among them will be all those of their an-

cestors who have died, their fathers, mothers, brothers, cousins and wives—all those who hear my voice and my words through the tongues of my children. I will cover the earth with new soil to a depth of five times the height of a man, and under this new soil will be buried the whites, and all the holes and the rotten places will be filled up. The new lands will be covered with sweetgrass and running water and trees, and herds of buffalo and ponies will stray over it, that my red children may eat and drink, hunt and rejoice. And the sea to the west I will fill up so that no ships may pass over it, and the other seas will I make impassable. And while I am making the new earth the Indians who have heard this message and who dance and pray and believe will be taken up in the air and suspended there, while the wave of new earth is passing; then set down among the ghosts of their ancestors, relatives, and friends. Those of my children who doubt will be left in undesirable places, where they will be lost and wander around until they believe and learn the songs and the dance of the ghosts. And while my children are dancing and making ready to join the ghosts, they shall have no fear of the white man, for I will take from the whites the secret of making gunpowder, and the powder they now have on hand will not burn when it is directed against the red people, my children, who know the songs and the dances of the ghosts; but that powder which my children, the red men, have, will bum and kill when it is directed against the whites and used by those who believe. And if a red man die at the hands of the whites while he is dancing, his spirit will only go to the end of the earth and there join the ghosts of his fathers and return to his friends next spring. Go then, my children, and tell these things to all the people and make all ready for the coming of the ghosts.'

"We were given food that was rich and sweet to taste, and as we sat there eating, there came up through the clouds a man, tall as a tree and thin like a snake, with great teeth sticking out of his mouth, his body covered with short hair, and we knew at once it was the Evil Spirit. And he said to the Great Spirit, 'I want half the people of the earth.' And the Great Spirit answered and said, 'No, I cannot give you any; I love them all too much.' The Evil Spirit asked again and was again refused, and asked the third time, and the Great Spirit then told him that he could have the whites to do what he liked with, but that he would not let him have any Indians, as they were his chosen people for all future time. Then we were shown the dances and taught the songs that I am bringing to you, my brothers, and were led down the ladder of clouds by him who had taken us up. We found our horses and rode back to the railroad, the Messiah flying along in the air with us and teaching us the songs for the new dances. At the railroad he left us and told us to return to our people, and tell them, and all the people of the red nations, what we had seen; and he promised us that he would return to the clouds no more, but would remain at the end of the earth and lead the ghosts of our fathers to meet us when the next winter is passed."

This relation—stripped of the flowers of language which even the less gifted of the Sioux medicine men use, and told as a bald and literal translation of what was a most attractive story to an imaginative and credulous people—was occasionally varied toward the end of Kicking Bear's mission, and he was known to have admitted that he did not make the journey to the clouds himself, but had met those who had gone aloft. These vagaries, however, did not count with those who had once committed themselves to the new faith. The doctrine was artfully framed to appeal to the cupidity of the Indian and to inflame him against the whites, carrying with it promise of return to the free life, with plenty of buffalo and no prospect of work. It upset none of the pagan ideas, and gave approval to the current belief in the existence of the ghosts. A more pernicious system of religion could not have been offered to a people who stood on the threshold of civilization, and who hungered for a realization of dreams that would free them from present poverty, probable hunger, and the prospect of toil.

The first thing to be done was to get rid of Kicking Bear. He was a big medicine man among his people, but I was convinced that Sitting Bull, having been initiated in the mysteries of the ghost-dance, would interpose no objection to the exclusion from his preserves of a competitor in the medicine-making. Sitting Bull had gone with zest into the business of promoting the new religion. Knowing his people, and utilizing the mysticism with which he habitually preyed on their superstitions, he established himself as the high priest of the cult even while Kicking Bear was still with him. He fasted and prayed with such vigor, and danced with such enthusiasm, that he reduced himself to mere skin and bone, and kept his people worked up to a high state of enthusiasm by inducing them to emulate his example. It was the appeal that the leaders of the ghost-dance made to the superstitions of the people that I feared most; and that I was justified in this fear was demonstrated when I sent a party of thirteen policemen, under the command of Crazy Walking, a man in whom I had the most complete faith, with orders to arrest Kicking Bear and eject him from the reservation.

The policemen found Kicking Bear and Sitting Bull conducting a seance, the Minniconjou exhorting the people. So impressed was the officer in charge of the police detachment with the dance and the wonderful stories told by the dancers about their visions, that he was turned from his purpose, and returned to the agency with Sitting Bull's promise that Kicking Bear would leave on the following day. This report was brought to me October 14, and I immediately sent Chatka, second lieutenant of the police force, to eject Kicking Bear. Lieutenant Chatka was a man of great firmness of character, and when he asked for only two men and said he would drive Kicking Bear out, I knew that the medicine of Kicking Bear would be wasted on him, whatever it might cost him mentally. Chatka arrived at Sitting Bull's camp on the Grand River the next day. A very large party of Indians were dancing. The lieutenant pushed his way through the dancers, notified Kicking Bear and six men from the Cheyenne River reservation who were with him, to leave the Standing Rock reservation forthwith, which they proceeded to do, and he conducted them to the Moreau River, the southern boundary of the reservation, about twenty-five miles southwest of Sitting Bull's camp. I cannot imagine a performance requiring more courage, from an Indian standpoint, than that accomplished by Lieutenant Chatka that day.

That night Sitting Bull broke the peace-pipe which he had kept sacredly since his surrender at Fort Buford in 1881. He deliberately broke it in the presence of the assemblage of ghost-dancers, saying that he was ready to fight and would die for this new religion if need be. The effect upon his over-credulous followers, of this grand-stand play, in which he was an adept, was, as the medicine man knew it would be, tremendous and far-reaching. The people understood Sitting Bull to mean that he would stand against the whites to the death; but he, at the same time, knew that the whites would pay no attention to this bit of bravado. After that day there was menace in the attitude of Sitting Bull that could only be met by summary treatment, and I recommended to the Department, urgently, the necessity of removing him, with his few mischief-making supporters, from the reservation to some remote military prison. I had previously, as early as June 18, 1890, made a similar recommendation, and included with him Circling Bear, Black Bird, and Circling Hawk, as men who should be removed from the reservation, whose active opposition to the government policies was detrimental to the peace and welfare of the Indians. At the same time I assured the Department of my control of the Indians on the reservation generally; and in this I was justified, for the disaffection never existed beyond about four hundred and fifty members, the immediate following of Sitting Bull, and thus involved only about ten percent of the Indians of the Standing Rock agency.

Sitting Bull became insolent to the Indian police, and arrogant through being left unmolested. The well-disposed Indians living along Grand River ad- jacent to his camp, who would not accept the absurdities of the new doctrine, were subjected to frequent insults from him and his fanatical crazed adherents. He kept his people madly engaged in the new dance, adding absurdities to it from time to time as he observed interest and enthusiasm among them lagging. His conduct and attitude for some weeks previous to his arrest, together with the mysteriousness of his nightly seances, to which only unwavering members of the new doctrine were admitted, with the further fact that his immediate followers were uncommunicative and sullen, made it plainly evident that he was secretly preparing for some rash movement."*

The inspector glanced outside his window, pondering how things could have turned out different for him and different for Sitting Bull and his people.

They were getting closer to Washington D.C. and the inspector was beginning to gain a clarity in the present through looking into the past for clues of what needed to be done. He began to understand what he would need to tell them about the gift of the waters. He knew he would tell the Vice President nearly the same thing he had said in his report, but he knew the Vice president would want to hear about the way the deal was made. And the deal was made the same way it had always been made and always will be made, through men.

He began to write again, trying to finish the thought he had started. He thought of his wife, Marie Louise, who had seen little of her husband in recent years. Thoughts of her flooded in his mind as he began to again write a story he would one day tell the world. Her feminine essence propelled him forward in a purity of mind and spirit.

THE DEATH OF SITTING BULL

*"That fall there were strenuous times on the

frontier, and, in the event, it marked the passing of that indefinable boundary between the refinements of civilization and the country to which the white man had turned in the determination to compel nature to his needs. Looking back at it now, I can see that the times were pregnant of great things. On the one hand stood the white man—and he was not standing still. Nothing could deter him from going forward, and if, in the march of civilization, a people was blotted out, it would not be the first time that the same march had proved remorseless.

On the other hand there was a people who stood at the threshold of civilization, many of whom were earnestly endeavoring to adjust themselves to the new conditions along the white man's road, but who wavered when bidden by the leaders of a savage cult to accept the new doctrine which so strongly appealed to all their traditions and inspirations. They were still very largely untutored, and strange to the ways of the white man. A few years back they knew no limit to their range in roaming save those set for them by tradition, and all of them remembered very vividly the buffalo and the plentitude of smaller game. The buffalo was as dependable and certain a means of subsistence for them as the crops of the white men,—even more so,—and in a day, almost, the buffalo had been obliterated. They had been accustomed to going out and taking what they would in the form of meat; suddenly that meat-supply was cut off, and they were rendered dependent on a government whose policy was the gradual reduction of gratuities to Indians. I was then, and am still, astonished at the spirit displayed by the Indians under the circumstances, and am sure it was not meekness. They were bold enough in most things, but they appeared to have been suddenly forced to the knowledge that the white man was master of the situation and the country, and that the salvation of the Indian lay along the broadly blazed trail made by the whites. The younger element among the Indians was quite ready to accept the inevitable, to abandon the god of things as they ought to be for "the god of things as they are." The unreconstructed element among the old leaders, who saw their power vanishing in the dawn of the day of the man who works, whose pride of place and chieftainship was being swallowed by Indians who had come to know the meaning of earning their bread by the sweat of their brows,—this element was standing for a voiceless and purposeless protest.

It was not to be wondered at that the unreconstructed Indians should seize upon the excuse furnished by the inventors of the Messianic movement to put their protest into form. Hollow Horn Bear, a chief of the Brule Sioux, and a man of standing and influence to-day, told me once that he saw the inevitable.

"I believe," he said, "that I must die, and I think it would be better for me to die fighting with weapons in my hands than to starve to death at the agency door."

Hollow Horn Bear has changed his opinion and his attitude, but what he said expressed the thought of the unreconstructed Indian of ghost-dancing days.

Considering the attitude of many of the older and more influential Indians and the seductive promises of the prophets of the Indian Messiah, it may be said now that a bloody Indian war was averted at that time by the narrowest margin, and that margin held by the men who had won the loyal support of Indians of standing and influence, whose intelligence had been developed to a stage which permitted them to see clearly that the Indian could not hope to cope with the white man in a test of strength. And, in my personal experience, I was shown that there were Indians whose loyalty to their pledged word was so strong and dependable that they were ready not only to dare the opprobrium of their people, but to defy the powers of the unseen and unknown world before which they and their ancestors had always trembled.

It was on the fidelity of such men as these that I reckoned when I assured the Department, in the summer of 1890, that there was no danger of an uprising and that I had my people well in hand. Going back to June 7 of that year, I find a letter from the Commissioner of Indian Affairs, in which it is stated that a letter had been received by the Department from a well- known citizen of Pierre, South Dakota, saying that the Sioux Indians were planning an outbreak. Replying to this letter I said, in part, under date of June 18:—

"So far as the Indians of this agency [Standing Rock] are concerned, there is nothing in either their words or their actions that would justify the rumor.... There are a few malcontents here, as at all of the Sioux agencies, who cling tenaciously to the old Indian ways and are slow to accept the new order of things,... and this class of Indians are ever ready to circulate idle rumors and sow dissensions to discourage the more progressive,... and the removal from among them of a few individuals such as Sitting Bull, Circling Bear, Black Bird, and Circling Hawk, of this agency, Big Foot and his lieutenants of Cheyenne River agency, Crow Dog and Low Dog of Rosebud, and any of the like sort of Pine Ridge, would end all trouble and uneasiness in the future."

This recommendation I reiterated repeatedly. It was the common-sense proposition to remove the disaffected from the well affected; but the desired order was not forthcoming until the disaffection had assumed alarming proportions. I felt secure in the knowledge that the Standing Rock Indians in general could be depended upon to behave themselves, but was very anxious that Sitting Bull, the prime mischief-maker, should be removed—not because there was danger that he might indulge in any overt act, but because he was demoralizing the people who submitted to his influence. The preachment to the Indians of this New Doctrine, and the possibilities of an unholy war based upon fanatical inspiration, was too good a thing to be passed by newspaper correspondents, and the public press soon announced with sensational headlines that the Messianic movement was quite general among the various Indian tribes, and had assumed startling proportions elsewhere before its effect was felt on the Standing Rock reservation.

The spread of news in the Indian country is one of those things not understandable of the white man, and the coming of the Messiah was spread among the Indians with the speed of the telegraph. It appeared one day among the Shoshones and Arapahoes in Wyoming, with a personal Messiah up in the mountains in some inaccessible place; the next day it was talked of in Oklahoma, Nebraska, North and South Dakota,—the Indians of widely distant localities coming simultaneously to the knowledge bf the impending emancipation of the red man. The preaching was varied according to the locality, or the needs or intelligence of its promoters and prophets. But behind it all there was the same menace to white domination, the same appeal to the prejudices and passions of the red man, the same promise of a return to the blissful state of freedom and plenty that had obtained before the coming of the white man and the passing of the buffalo. In those parts of the country where the Indian was as little understood as he was known personally, his mysterious attitude led many to believe it to mean an impending Indian war, and everybody appeared to overlook the conditions that surrounded the red man. If it had developed a war, it could only have been a war of self-sacrifice, resulting in extermination of the Indians involved, as it could not have gone further than outbreaks in certain sections of the country, as, for instance, among the allied people of what had recently been the Great Sioux reservation. An outbreak might be disastrous if the Indians were permitted to mass, after defying the agency authorities, but only sparsely settled districts would be involved. It was plainly the business of the government and its agents to prevent the Indians from leaving the reservations upon which they were located, and to suppress the ghost-dancing by demonstrating to the unthinking the powerlessness of their prophets to save themselves from punishment for insubordination. I knew these conditions, and suggested a remedy at once in the removal of the trouble-makers.

I had no doubt of the loyalty of a vast majority of the people of the reservation, and knew that the suppression of the "pernicious activity" of Sitting Bull would go far toward putting an end to the craze throughout the country; but he was not removed and became bolder in his work of spreading the ghost-dancing propaganda. His following, however, continued very generally restricted to his own particular people of the Hunkpapa band living along the Grand River. But some of the best men on the reservation were touched in their superstitious natures by the new religion. I had to bolster up more than one of the head men, and in this I was aided by their personal hatred of the man who had led them into so much trouble in the seventies. There were not wanting those who volunteered to go out and bring Sitting Bull in; but, lacking orders for the arrest of the man, I could not permit this.

October 17 I wrote the Department again, giving a history of the ghost-dancing craze on the Standing Rock reservation, and concluding in these words:—

"Desiring to exhaust all reasonable means before resorting to extremes, I have sent a message to Sitting Bull, by One Bull, his nephew, that I want to see him at the agency, and I feel quite confident that I shall succeed in allaying the present excitement and put a stop to this absurd craze for the present at least; but I would respectfully recommend the removal from the reservation and confinement in some military prison at a distance from the Sioux country, of Sitting Bull and the parties named in my letter of June 18 last." In response to this I received, under date of October 29, a letter from Acting Commissioner of Indian Affairs, R. V. Belt, directing me to notify Sitting Bull and the other malcontents that the Secretary of the Interior was greatly displeased with their conduct, and to let Sitting Bull understand that he would be held to a strict accountability for the misconduct of any of his followers. During the following two weeks agitation was progressing in the outside world and the state of the public mind was probably represented in the action of the government which resulted in this order by telegraph:—

"WASHINGTON, Nov. 14, 1890. "To MCLAUGH-LIN, "Agent, Standing Rock Agency,— "The President has directed the Secretary of War to assume a military responsibility for the suppression of any threatened outbreak among the Sioux Indians, and that an officer of high rank be sent to investigate the situation among them. He suggests that the agents separate the well-disposed from the ill-disposed Indians, and, while maintaining their control and discipline, so far as possible to avoid forcing any issue that will result in an outbreak. You will exercise wise discretion in carrying out the President's suggestion, carefully observing the caution he directs and avoiding publicity of these instructions. "R. V. Belt, "Acting Commissioner."

At this late day I am frank to say that I feared military interference with the Indians, not that I doubted the capacity of the military, but because I was convinced that a military demonstration would precipitate a collision and bloodshed, which might be avoided. I was on excellent terms with all of the army officers of the Department of Dakota, and Colonel Drum, the commanding officer at Fort Yates, was quite as anxious as I was that Sitting Bull and his lieutenants should be quietly removed from the reservation, we continuing to cooperate during the ghost-dancing and up to the time of its culmination.

Things went on as usual in the Messianic camp, the Indians dancing, with Sitting Bull making medicine daily and promising the extermination of the whites, until November 17, when I proceeded, in company with Louis Primeau, a mixed-blood interpreter, to the Grand River, where I was informed a big dance was in progress. At this time Sitting Bull had not been in for his rations for some weeks, which led me to believe that he meant mischief. I had always made it a practice to go unarmed among the Indians, and the fact that I carried no arms that day, and the further fact that I was on excellent terms, personally, with nearly all the Indians, doubtless stood me in good stead.

I arrived at Sitting Bull's camp about three o'clock in the afternoon. It was Sunday, and I was not surprised to see a large gathering of people in front of the houses, six in number, in the centre of the camp. Many of the Indians had come on a visit, but they had brought their tents with them as though to make a prolonged stay. Having approached the camp by a road not usually traveled, and my coming being unexpected, I found the ghost-dance at its full height. There were about two hundred people standing in a circle about the dancers, and except for a few men who endeavored to avoid being seen by me, I received no attention from the enthusiasts as I approached. But the madness of the dance demonstrated the height of distraction to which the dancers had attained.

The sacred pole about which the people danced was set some distance from the houses. Around this pole a ring of men, women, boys, and girls, about one hundred in all, were dancing. Some of the younger ones had been pupils of the reservation day schools until within a few weeks. The dancers held each other's hands, and were all jumping madly, whirling to the left about the pole, keeping time to a mournful crooning song, that sometimes rose to a shriek as the women gave way to the stress of their feelings. There was nothing of the slow and precise treading which ordinarily marks the time of the Indian religious dance. Some of the dancers had thrown off their upper clothing, and all were gasping excitedly; a few who had been dancing for a considerable length of time were completely crazed, with their tongues lolling from their mouths. Occasionally a poor creature, overcome by the fatigue of the exciting dance, would fall out of the ring, which was immediately closed up, and the circling to the left continued, the dancers paying no attention to the fallen one. As I looked on, a middle- aged woman fell out of the circle and rolled to some distance. She was picked up by the shoulders by two Indians, whose trappings indicated that they were officers of the dance, and who dragged her to a tepee which I had not noticed before, but which commanded my attention now, for within the wide-open flaps of the wigwam, seated on a sort of throne, was my old friend, Sitting Bull. He was very much thinner than a few weeks previous, but the look he gave me showed that his wits were not dulled or his hatred and envy lessened by the rigor of his life. By his side, fantastically dressed, stood Bull Ghost, Sitting Bull's mouthpiece in the ghost-dance exercises. Bull Ghost had been rather popular with the whites around the agency, and was familiarly known as 'One-Eyed-Riley,' he having but one eye and that not an attractive orb.

The woman, still in a swoon, was laid at Sitting Bull's feet, and Bull Ghost announced in a loud voice that she was in a trance and communicating with the ghosts, upon which announcement the dance ceased, so that the dancers might hear the message from the spirit world. Sitting Bull performed certain incantations, then leaned over and put his ear to the woman's lips. He spoke in a low voice to his herald, Bull Ghost, who repeated to the listening multitude the message which Sitting Bull pretended to receive from the unconscious woman. Sitting Bull had all the tricks of the fake spiritualist. Knowing his people intimately, he knew all about the dead relatives of the woman who had fainted, and he made a tremendous impression on his audience by giving them personal messages from the Indian ghosts, who announced with great unanimity that they were marching east to join their living kinsmen the following spring.

The excitement was very intense, the people being brought to a pitch of high nervousness by the treatment prescribed by Sitting Bull for his followers. He required that each initiate, as well as those desiring to join the ghost-dancers, take a vapor-bath every morning, and this was accomplished by means of small, closely built lodges, in which the people collected, three or four at a time. Outside of the lodge a hole was dug in the ground, in which attendants heated small boulders, and thrust them into the lodge, together with a bucket of water, then closed all openings of the wickiup. The hot stones were sprinkled with water, thus creating a hot steam in the small lodge, and during this bath prayers were being sung continually. The bathers remained in the steam- heated tent as long as they could stand it, and were then dragged forth, nearly dead, to be anointed by the medicine man and then permitted to dance until they dropped; and this daily performance, with very little food, had made them subjects for the madhouse.

Obviously there would be no sense in attempting to talk to them in their present state, and I drove off to Bull Head's house, three miles away.

At daylight next morning, I returned to Sitting Bull's camp. It was barely six o'clock when I arrived, Bull Head, Lieutenant of the Indian Police, riding beside the wagon in which Primeau and I rode. The camp was very quiet, but there were figures about the long row of wickiups in which the ghost-dancers were taking their vapor-baths. I entered Sitting Bull's house and found his two wives and four of his children within. The women, very much excited, said that Sitting Bull was taking a bath, and offered to go and call him. They were told not to disturb him, as I would wait until he had finished his bath; and after conversing with the family a few minutes, I left the house. As I turned the corner of the building, I came face to face with the old medicine man, who had seen me entering his cabin and came to learn why I was so early abroad. He was naked, but for a breech-cloth and moccasins, and he looked very thin and more subdued than I had ever seen him. He stopped and said, "How."

"How," said I, and extended my hand, which he took, and I drew him toward the wagon and away from the cabin. He was handed a blanket, which he gathered around him, and stopped, sullen, but not fiercely inso-lent, as he had been with white people since the dancing had commenced. Other figures crept out of the wickiups in the early morning light and began to gather around us. Sitting Bull said nothing, and I made up my mind that I would proceed at once to tell him what I had to say before the entire encampment could congregate and disturb us. "Look here, Sitting Bull," I began, "I want to know what you mean by your present conduct and ut-ter disregard of department orders. Your preaching and practicing of this absurd Messiah doctrine is causing a great deal of uneasiness among the Indians of the reser-vation, and you should stop it at once."

He was actually meek, and I thought perhaps he

might be sincere in his religious fervor; but his crafty eye dispelled that idea. Without giving him time to talk, I recalled all my connection with him and showed him my friendly inclination. I recalled the time when he had sent word to me from Alberta, Canada, by Bishop Marty, to help him make his peace with the authorities before he surrendered; I reminded him of the talk we had when he was a prisoner on the steamer General Sherman, leaving Fort Yates for Fort Randall in September, 1881, and how he had been given his liberty through following my advice. He mumbled some thanks when I told him of the time he had written to me from Fort Randall, and sent the letter by his brother-in-law, Gray Eagle, and adopted brother, Little Assiniboine, in which he had besought me to try and obtain his freedom and have him sent to Standing Rock reservation. And I went on, Indian- like, through the little list of things I had done for him at various times, and wound up by reproaching him for leading the people astray and setting them back for years, besides making it certain that they would all be punished. His eyes flashed, but the old fellow did not break out in a rage as I expected he might. On the contrary he seemed to be impressed at once, and when Yellow Otter's voice rose loud in excited protest, above the sneering of the crowd that had gathered about us, he turned on the speaker and ordered him to be silent. Then he indulged in a harangue. He spoke only of the new faith, and how he believed in it and the good that it would bring to his people. I interrupted him to say that it would bring them all into trouble, and that he well knew it to be rubbish. He grew a little defiant and told me that I knew nothing about it. Then he changed his tune and said:—

"Father, I will make you a proposition which will

settle this question. You go with me to the agencies to the West, and let me seek for the men who saw the Messiah; and when we find them, I will demand that they show him to us, and if they cannot do so I will return and tell my people it is a lie."

I told him that such an attempt would be like catching up with the wind that blew last year; that he should come and spend a night with me at the agency, so that I might convince him of the absurdity of the doctrine he was practicing, through which he was misleading his over-credulous followers.

This he would not do, but said:—

"My heart inclines to do what you request, but I must consult my people. I would be willing to go with you now, but I cannot leave without the consent of my people. I will talk to the men to-night, and if they think it advisable I will go to the agency next Saturday."

I could get no further promise from him, and drove away, the crowd threatening and sneering, but held in check by the upraised arm of the old medicine man, standing almost naked in the bright but chilly morning sunlight. Our talk had lasted about an hour, and I said nothing to Primeau, who accompanied me, nor did Primeau make any remark as we drove out of the camp, but I know that we both felt more comfortable when we got over a ridge of hills and out of rifle-range of the crazed throng of ghost-dancers.

That was the last time that I saw Sitting Bull alive, for he sent word by Strikes-the-Kettle the following Saturday that he could not come to the agency.

I reported this visit to the Department, and, being quite convinced that Sitting Bull would not come in, I wrote, under date of November 19, recommending that the ghost-dancers be attacked in the weakest point of their religious armor—through their stomachs. My recommendation was that all Indians living on Grand River be notified that those wishing to be known as opposed to the ghost-doctrine, friendly to the government, and desiring the support provided for in the treaty, should report at the agency for enrollment and be required to encamp near the agency for a few weeks, and that subsistence issues be withheld from those electing to remain on Grand River, continuing their medicine practices in violation of department orders. I was quite confident that such a course would soon have left Sitting Bull with but few followers, as all, or nearly all, would have reported for enrollment and rations, and he would thus have been forced to come in himself.

I had no doubt then and have none now that, if this suggestion had been adopted, the ghost-dancing would have been broken up, for I knew the Indian well enough to be assured that a material meal would attract him far more effectually than a feast with the ghosts. The suggestion was not officially adopted, but events were crowding at Washington, and November 20 I received this telegram:—

"MCLAUGHLIN, Agent,— "If condition of affairs now and for future requires that leaders of excitement or fomenters of disturbance should be arrested and confined to insure quiet and good order among Indians, telegraph me names at once, so that assistance of military while , operating to suppress any attempted outbreak may be had to make arrests. "R. V. Belt, "Acting Commissioner."

I wired the names of the men whose arrest I had suggested the preceding June, adding the names of Iron White Man and Male Bear, but added that I thought it imprudent to attempt making the desired arrests at that time, and invited attention to my suggestion of the 19th.

At that time the situation was well in hand, and if I could have chosen the time I could have arrested Sitting Bull without bloodshed. The plan was simple enough, it being the custom of the Indians of the entire reservation to congregate at the agency once every two weeks (every alternate Saturday), to receive their rations, and on these issue-days Sitting Bull was practically alone at his camp on Grand River, forty miles from the agency. The police, under Lieutenant Bull Head, were absolutely to be depended upon and willing to do anything that would promote order. Lieutenant Bull Head, who lived about three miles west of the ghost-dance camp, was watching Sitting Bull and his followers and kept them under strict surveillance. The old chief could make no move that could not be anticipated, and the arrest could be made without difficulty, unless trouble was precipitated from the outside. And the threat came on us like a bolt from the blue, and though bloodshed was averted for the moment, I knew that affairs might get beyond control at any time.

The threat took form in Colonel William F. Cody (Buffalo Bill), who arrived at the agency on November 28, with an order signed by General Miles, then division commander, directing military officers to supply Colonel Cody with whatever assistance was necessary in arresting Sitting Bull. It was not my affair, but I felt that I was responsible for the conduct of the Indians, and I knew that any attempt by outside parties to arrest Sitting Bull would undoubtedly result in loss of life, as the temper of the ghost-dancers was not to be doubted. And upon Colonel Cody's arrival at the agency I sent the following telegram to Washington:—

"COMMISSIONER OF INDIAN AFFAIRS,— "William F. Cody (Buffalo Bill) has arrived here with commission from Gen. Miles to arrest Sitting Bull. Such a step at present is unnecessary and unwise, as it will precipitate a fight which can be averted. A few Indians still dancing, but it does not mean mischief at present. I have matters well in hand, and when proper time arrives can arrest Sitting Bull by Indian police without bloodshed. I ask attention to my letter of November 19. Request Gen. Miles's order to Cody be rescinded and request immediate answer. "MCLAUGHLIN, Agent."

I felt that I was justified in asking that the order of a general of division, who was not on the ground, should be rescinded. It was a bold step to take, but I could see nothing else to do. And I was still convinced that the arrest would be bloodless only if made on ration-day. The morning after Colonel Cody's arrival he left the agency with a civilian escort for Sitting Bull's camp before any reply had been received to my telegram of the previous day. I had no disposition to interpose my feeble authority to that of the military, on the contrary I had been cooperating fully with Colonel Drum, the commandant at Fort Yates; but my telegram saved to the world that day a royal good fellow and most excellent showman, for General Miles's order was rescinded by telegraph, and Buffalo Bill was overtaken with the message and turned back before he reached Grand River.

The Buffalo Bill incident was hardly disposed

of before it was made clear that the future operations against the ghost-dancers were to be carried on at the direction of the military arm, and on December 1, 1 received this telegram:—

"WASHINGTON, Dec.1. "MCLAUGHLIN, Agent, "Standing Rock,— "By direction of the Secretary, during the present Indian troubles, you are instructed that while you shall continue all the business and carry into effect the educational and other purposes of your agency, you will, as to all operations intended to suppress any outbreak by force, cooperate with and obey the orders of the military officers commanding on the reservation in your charge. "R. V. Belt, "Acting Commissioner."

It was evident that the military intended to arrest Sitting Bull, and I still had it in my mind that if I could make provision to make the arrest by the Indian police, at an opportune time and in my own way, there would be no necessity for shedding blood. I was absolutely convinced that, unless the arrest was made by surprise, there would be trouble. I telegraphed the commissioner December 6, again, asking if I was authorized to arrest Sitting Bull when I thought best, and got this reply:—

"WASHINGTON, Dec. 6. "MCLAUGHLIN, Agent,— "Replying to your telegram of this date, Secretary directs that you make no arrests whatever, except under orders of the military, or upon an order from the Secretary of the Interior. "R. V. Belt, "Acting Commissioner."

General Ruger, then in command of the Department of Dakota, showed the utmost good-will and a desire to cooperate with the agency people, as the following telegram, referring to a message sent by him to Colonel Drum, the commanding officer at Fort Yates, demonstrates:—

"ST. PAUL, MINN., Dec. 6. "U. S. Indian Agent, James McLaughlin,—"Referring to telegram sent to Col. Drum, which he will show you, is there any change of condition recently which makes present action specially necessary? As you know I am disposed to support you. Some prior movements I would like to see completed. "RUGER, "Brigadier General, Commanding."

In reply I telegraphed General Huger that there had been no material change in conditions; that the police could keep Sitting Bull on the reservation and arrest him when necessary, but that there was no urgent need for action. It was too late for action that day—which was beef-ration day—and I was still minded to stick to my original proposition that the arrest should be made while Sitting Bull was practically alone at his camp. He had not been in for his rations since October 25. The dancing was still going on, with cold weather—so usual at that season of the year, and which might have been depended on to cool the ardor of the dancers—still holding off.

Sitting Bull was in constant communication with the Southern Sioux agencies, and it was becoming very certain that he was going to attempt to leave the reservation, and his escape had to be guarded against. The disaffected Indians at the agencies along the Missouri River, as well as those of Rosebud and Pine Ridge, would see in him a leader they might follow to a desperate purpose, and I was not going to permit him to decamp. In the Bad Lands there was gathered a considerable mass of Indians, eighteen hundred having stampeded from their homes when General Brook arrived at Pine Ridge with five companies of infantry and three troops of cavalry, part of which force he detached and sent to Rosebud. Big Foot and his band escaped after arrest by the military on the Cheyenne River reservation. Obviously it would not do to allow so cunning and malignant a leader as Sitting Bull to put himself at the head of these frightened or desperate people. There is no doubt that many of the Indians who had taken to the Bad Lands were simply frightened by the presence of the troops. But they were also tremendously excited, and in their stampede and flight destroyed much property belonging to themselves and others. I knew that Sitting Bull contemplated putting himself at the head of the fugitives, and that those who were merely frightened would soon be turned or coerced to acts of hostility under his guidance.

Ninety percent of the Standing Rock Indians continued loyal, the police were devoted and vigilant, and only the Sitting Bull following gave promise of trouble. December 12 came the order for the arrest of Sitting Bull. It was in the form of a cipher telegram and follows, translated:—

"To COMMANDING OFFICER, "Fort Yates, N. D.,— "The division commander has directed that you make it your especial duty to secure the person of Sitting Bull. Call on Indian agent to cooperate and render such assistance as will best promote the purpose in view. Acknowledge receipt, and if not perfectly clear, repeat back. "M. BARBER, "Assistant Adjutant General. "DEPARTMENT OF DAKOTA, "ST. PAUL, MINN., Dec. 12, 1890."

Colonel Drum furnished me with a copy of the order, and upon conferring with him in reference to the arrest, we fully agreed on the course of procedure. Colonel Drum was quite of the same mind that I was about the necessity for making the arrest while Sitting Bull's camp was practically deserted; that it should be made by the Indian police, with the military supporting at a convenient distance, to aid the police in case of attempted rescue, and it was finally determined that the arrest should be made on the next ration-day, December 20, unless it was precipitated by Sitting Bull trying to leave the reservation. Lieutenant Bull Head, of the Indian police, who lived, as I have said, about three miles west of the ghost-dance camp, was given charge of the duty of keeping Sitting Bull under surveillance, with orders instantly to report any suspicious movements. He chose for his assistant First Sergeant Shave Head, a stouthearted and intelligent man who could be depended upon in any emergency. They were to hold a considerable force of Indian police on the Grand River, adjacent to Sitting Bull's camp, and Sergeant Eagle- man was sent with eight additional policemen to Oak Creek, twenty miles south of the agency, that they might be within supporting distance if needed by the force on Grand River.

About six o'clock in the evening of December 13, Bull Ghost came into the agency with a letter to me from Sitting Bull, his last utterance, full of defiance and implied threats, but so incoherent as to be difficult to understand. It was written by Andrew Fox, Sitting Bull's son-in-law, who could speak English and write a little. It was addressed, "The Major at the Indian office." These portions I could decipher:—

"I had a meeting with all my Indians today and am writing this order to you.... God made the red race and the white, but the white higher.... I wish no one to come to me in my prayers with gun or knife.

...And you, my friend, today you think I am foil

[fool] and you tell some of the wise men among my people... so you don't like me.... I don't like myself, my friend, when someone is foil.... You think if I am not here the Indians is civilization.... Also I will let you know something. I got to go to Pine Ridge agency, and to know this pray. So I let you know that and the policeman told me that you going to take all our ponies, guns too. So I want to let you know this. I want answer back soon.

"SITTING BULL."

While Sitting Bull was having this letter written, he was preparing to leave the reservation and his horses had been brought in. On the 14th, in the afternoon, special policeman Hawk Man brought me a letter from Bull Head, dated at Grand River at 12.50 a m., and written by John M. Carignan, then teacher at the Grand River day-school, now manager of a trader's store at Fort Yates, informing me that Sitting Bull was getting ready to leave the reservation and action must be taken at once; that his horses had been doing nothing for several weeks, being well fed all the time; and that, being thus better mounted than the Indian police, if he got started, they would be unable to overtake the party or prevent them from reaching the Bad Lands, where the main body of the disaffected Sioux had congregated. Colonel Drum, the post commander, having seen the courier passing his quarters, and being anxious to learn the latest news from the Sitting Bull camp, came into my office while I was reading the letter, and upon being informed of its contents concluded that the arrest should be made the next morning. I was anxious that the arrest should be made by the police, because otherwise it was not possible without bloodshed; and for the further reason that the arrest being made by the police would have a salutary effect upon the Indians in general. Colonel Drum heartily agreed with me in this view of the case, and it was determined that two troops of the Eighth Cavalry, numbering one hundred men, with Captain E. G. Fechet in command, should leave Fort Yates at midnight in order to arrive at the Oak Creek crossing of the Sitting Bull road by 6.30 of the 15th, to support the police if necessary; and before Colonel Drum left my office, I wrote the following letter in English, with a translation of it in Sioux, ordering the arrest of Sitting Bull, which I sent to Lieutenant Bull Head by Second Sergeant Red Tomahawk.

"STANDING ROCK AGENCY, N.D., "Dec. 14, 1890. "Lieut. Bull Head, or Sergt. Shave Head, "Grand River,— "

From reports brought by Scout Hawk Man I believe that the time has arrived for the arrest of Sitting Bull and that it can be made by the Indian police without much risk. I therefore desire you to make the arrest before daylight tomorrow morning, and try and get back to the Sitting Bull road crossing of Oak Creek by daylight tomorrow morning or as soon thereafter as possible. The Cavalry will leave tonight and reach the Sitting Bull crossing of Oak Creek before daylight tomorrow morning (Mon- day), where they will remain until they hear from you.

"Louis Primeau will accompany the Cavalry command as guide, and I desire you to send a messenger to the Cavalry as soon as you can after making the arrest, so that the troops may know how to act in aiding you or preventing any attempt of his followers from rescuing him. "I have ordered all the police at Oak Creek to

proceed to Carignan's school and await your orders. This gives you a force of forty-two policemen for the arrest.
"Very respectfully,
"JAMES MCLAUGHLIN, "U. S. Indian Agent.
"P. S. You must not let him escape under any circumstances."

These orders, in duplicate, were, as before stated, given to Sergeant Red Tomahawk, a man who could be depended upon to get through with them, and who did so and signally distinguished himself the next morning. The verbal instructions given Red Tomahawk as to assembling the scattered detachments of the Indian police were complete.

Thirty-nine regular policemen and four specials, under Bull Head and Shave Head, rode into the Sitting Bull camp at early dawn the next morning. Some of the men had traveled immense distances to rendezvous at the home of Lieutenant Bull Head, and all were firmly determined to make the arrest. Sitting Bull's band lived in houses stretching along the Grand River for a distance of four or five miles. About the home of the chief, consisting of two houses and a corral, there were a half-dozen log-cabins of good size. Many of the houses were deserted, the Indians having been engaged in dancing the greater part of the previous night. The entrance of the policemen awakened the camp, but they saw no one, as Bull Head wheeled his men between the Sitting Bull houses and ordered them to dismount. Ten policemen, headed by Bull Head and Shave Head, entered one of the houses, eight policemen the other. In the house entered by Bull Head's party they found the old medicine man, his two wives, and Crow Foot his son, a youth of seventeen years.

The women were very much frightened and began to cry. Sitting Bull sat up and asked what was the matter.

"You are under arrest and must go to the agency," said Bull Head. "Very well," said Sitting Bull, "I will go with you." And he told one of his wives to go to the other house and bring him his best clothes. He showed no concern at his arrest, but evidently wanted to make a good impression and dressed himself with some care. He had also asked that his best horse, a gray one, be saddled, and an Indian policeman had the animal at the door by the time Sitting Bull was dressed and ready to leave.

There had been no trouble in the house, and the police, when they walked out, were surprised at the extent of the demonstration. They came out of the building in a little knot, Bull Head on one side of Sitting Bull, Shave Head on the other, and Red Tomahawk directly behind. They had been twenty minutes or more in Sitting Bull's house, and it was in the gray of the morning when they came out. They stepped out into a mass of greatly excited ghost-dancers, nearly all armed and crowding about the main body of the police, who had held the way clear at the door. As Sitting Bull stepped out with his captors he walked directly toward the horse, with the evident intention of mounting and accompanying the police. He was some distance from the door when his son, Crow Foot, seeing that the old man intended to make no resistance, began to revile him:—

"You call yourself a brave man and you have declared that you would never surrender to a blue-coat, and now you give yourself up to Indians in blue uniforms," the young man shouted.

The taunt hit Sitting Bull hard. He looked into the mass of dark, excited faces, and commenced to talk volubly and shrilly, and there was a menacing movement in the crowd.

The last moment of Sitting Bull's life showed him in a better light, so far as physical courage goes, than all the rest of it. He looked about him and saw his faithful adherents—about one hundred and sixty crazed ghost-dancers—who would have gone through fire at his bidding; to submit to arrest meant the end of his power and his probable imprisonment; he had sure news from Pine Ridge that he, only, was needed to head the hostiles there in a war of extermination against the white settlers. He made up his mind to take his chance, and screamed out an order to his people to attack the police.

Instantly Catch-the-Bear and Strikes-the-Kettle, who were in the front rank of the crowd, fired at point-blank range, Catch-the-Bear mortally wounding First Lieutenant Bull Head, and Strikes-the-Kettle shooting First Sergeant Shave Head in the abdomen. Lieutenant Bull Head was a few yards to the left and front of Sitting Bull when hit, and immediately wheeling, he shot Sitting Bull through the body, and at the same instant Second Sergeant Red Tomahawk, who with revolver in hand was rear-guard, shot him in the right cheek, killing him instantly; the lieutenant, the first sergeant, and Sitting Bull falling together.

Sitting Bull's medicine had not saved him, and the shot that killed him put a stop forever to the domination of the ancient regime among the Sioux of the Standing Rock reservation.

The tale of the bloody fight that ensued has been told, and the world knows how those thirty-nine Indian policemen, with four of their relatives who volunteered to accompany them,—a total of forty- three in all,—fought off one hundred and sixty ghost-dancers, eight of whom were killed and five wounded; how second Sergeant Red Tomahawk, after the two higher ranking police officers had been mortally wounded, took command and drove the Indians to the timber; how Hawk Man No. 1 ran through a hail of bullets to get the news to the cavalry detachment, and how six faithful friends of the whites, policemen of the Standing Rock reservation, laid down their lives in doing their duty that morning. Two days later, on December 17, 1890, we buried Shave Head and four other Indian policemen with military honors in the cemetery at Standing Rock, and, while Captain Miner's entire company of the Twenty-Second U. S. Infantry fired three volleys over the graves of these red heroes, and a great concourse of the Sioux of the reservation stood in the chill bright sunlight of a fair winter's day, mourning aloud for their dead, I quietly left the enclosure and joined a little burial-party in the military cemetery at Fort Yates, situated situated about five hundred yards south of the agency cemetery. Four military prisoners dug the grave, and in the presence of A. R. Chapin, Assistant Surgeon, U. S. A., H. M. Deeble, Acting Assistant Surgeon, U. S. A., Lieutenant P. G. Wood, U. S. A., Post Quartermaster, now Brigadier General, retired, and myself, the body of Sitting Bull, wrapped in canvas and placed in a coffin, was lowered into the grave."*

A tear gently flowed from McLaughlin's eye as he wrote the last word of his recollection of the arrest of Sitting Bull. It had been almost six years since that fateful day. There hadn't been a single day he hadn't thought about what became of his friend and the great medicine man that was Sitting Bull.

He knew now what he would tell the Vice President and it would be different from the times before. He would avoid a disaster like that which befell Sitting Bull and the Sioux, who were deprived of their land and the love they held for it.

Chief Washakie and Sharp Nose were two different chiefs, from two different tribes. They were forced together by the hand of the government and the purchase of the waters would not have happened if he had not traveled with the two tribes through the land and listened to their wisdom and knowledge of the land.

McLaughlin learned from experience that he would have to gain the trust of the two elder chiefs in order to broker a deal. In order to broker a deal in Washington, he would have to use all the skills at his disposal to convey the true essence of the land and the people that inhabited them.

The train whistle sounded off as it pulled into the station. Passengers began to collect their belongings, stiffened from sitting so long. McLaughlin collected himself and stood confidently, moving in stride for what stood before him in the not-so-distant future. He had come to peace with the past only after letting it destroy him, building himself up with the distraction of some new to be tragedy.

Trust is Earned

McLaughlin stood before a delegation of men, the Vice President the most notable.

"Gentleman," McLaughlin said in a raised voice, commanding the room. "We are gathered here to discuss the acquisition of 10 miles square of land in the state of Wyoming from the Arapahoe and Shoshone reservation. I have before you an official transcript of the treaty which was signed on April 20, 1896. A total of 273 inhabitants of the reservation were in attendance for the treaty.

The Assistant Secretary of the interior began to read the transcript:

*At a council held at the Shoshone Agency council room by and between James McLaughlin, United States Indian Inspector, on the part of the United States, and Chiefs Washakie, of the Shoshones, and Sharp Nose, of the Arapahoes, and other head men of the Shoshone and Arapahoe tribes of Indians occupying the Shoshone Reservation, in the State of Wyoming, with Norkok and, Edmore Le Clair, Shoshone interpreters, and Henry Bee and William Shakespeare, Arapahoe interpreters, the following proceedings were had, to wit:

Capt. Richard H. Wilson, Eighth Infantry, acting Indian Agent, called the council to order at 10:30 a.m. and said:

"For a long while the Shoshones and Arapahoes have asked me to write to the Great Father about selling the Big Horn Hot Springs. I did write, and he has sent Inspector McLaughlin here to talk to you about it. He is a good friend to the Indians; was agent twenty-four years for the Sioux, and will tell you all about it. He will now speak to you," Wilson said.

"My friends, Shoshones and Arapahoes, I am pleased to see so many of you here today. I call you friends, because I come among you as a friend of the Indians. I am exceedingly anxious that I will be understood by the Indians in this council, and also that I will understand what the Indians wish to convey to me through their interpreters, and therefore I expect the assistant interpreters to rectify - any mistakes that the official interpreters may make. I have been sent by the Secretary of the Interior to confer with you, the Shoshones and Arapahoes, regarding the cession of a small tract of your reservation. The Secretary of the Interior represents the Great Father in Indian matters, and I was directed by him to visit the northeastern corner of the reservation, which embraces the Big Horn Hot Springs, with the view of purchasing it from you. Therefore my business here is to have you cede a small portion of your reservation embracing this spring, and as that is my chief business here, I wish to confine the present meeting strictly to that business, After that has been settled then I will with pleasure listen to any other business you may wish to bring before me. I made my visit to the springs that I might be the better enabled to report upon the character of the country and the advisability of having that tract purchased by the Government and set apart as a national park or reservation to be under Government control, and that that portion around the springs may be improved by giving bath houses, hotels, and other conveniences erected for the accommodation of the general public and they establishment of a health resort," McLaughlin said.

"As the Government will have absolute control of these springs you Indians will have the same privileges to use them as the public generally. As they now are they bring you in no revenue or return, and while they remain unimproved they will never be of any value to you. You all know the country surrounding the springsIs very poor and very few of you Indians ever visit it, and as all the game has disappeared from that section of country it is of very little value to you now. The sale of this piece of land, which I am authorized to negotiate with you for, and for which I am prepared to pay you liberally, will not affect your reservation except to enhance value of the remaining portion. (At this point there was considerable said by the Indians among themselves to clearly understand this). I desire to negotiate for a cession of 10 miles square, that is, commencing at the northeastern corner of the reservation, where Owl Creek empties into the Big Horn River; thence 10 miles south following the eastern boundary of the reservation; thence due west 10 miles; thence due north to the middle of the channel of Owl Creek, which forms a portion of the northern boundary of the reservation; thence following the middle of the channel of Owl Creek to the point of beginning.

"Here the map of Wyoming, showing the reservation, colored red, was exhibited, and the location and size of the desired tract was pointed out to the Indians.

Inspector McLaughlin said that his letter of instructions directed him to visit the springs and, after having collected such further information regarding them as might be necessary to a thorough understanding of the situation, he was to call a general council of the Indians belonging to the reservation and present to them the question of ceding the lands embracing said springs to the United States, and if, as it appeared from information in possession of the Department, the country in the vicinity of the springs was of little value, then the springs themselves would be the principal item of value to enter into the consideration.

"I was directed to explain to you that it was the purpose of the Government to enact appropriate legislation forever reserving the springs for the use and benefit of the general public; that it was proposed to erect suitable - buildings and provide other necessary facilities for bathing: and that. the Indians would be allowed to enjoy the advantages of these conveniences with the public generally.

"The Government does not expect to gain anything by this purchase, and, instead a large sum of money will have to be expended to improve the place. Now, having explained my mission, I wish to know whether you are ready to dispose of this tract of land. I now await your decision as to whether you wish to dispose of it or not. If you do, I will make you a proposition," McLaughlin finished.

Chief Washakie, of the Shoshones, arose and

said: "Now you will hear what I have to say. A good many years ago I used to live near Fort Bridger, called Piney. Then there was a man like you came to me and asked me, 'Where is your country? Where is your country? Is it here, or there, or in several places?' (Points to the north, south, east, and west.) I did not say anything. He stopped one night, and the next day I said, It is not here, meaning Piney, it is over the mountains, where the hot springs are, meaning both hot springs.

"After I got here I stayed here. After the game was gone then I told my agent to write to Washington. I want to sell those springs. I used to go to the hot springs on Owl Creek when the game and buffalo were there, and stay there. When buffalo were plenty I wintered there. Now I have moved away from there and have come over in this country. I was afraid to stay there when there was nothing to eat. I came here to farm a little. One hot spring (meaning a large hot spring near the agency) is enough for me, my people, and my soldiers. The soldiers just the same as own the spring, I listen to what Washington says, and I try to obey his orders. That is the reason that when the allotting agent, Colonel Clark, came here and the Indians did not want to survey their land, I told my men to have their land surveyed, and I have tried to do right just what Washington wants me to do. My land is pretty large, It is not small, and I have not stolen it. My friends that spoke for and secured this land are all dead and gone. I am the only one of the old men of my people left. I came here, and I have stayed here. You have never heard of Washakie doing anything wrong. Have you ever heard of Washakie doing anything wrong?" Washakie asked.

"I have never heard anything but good of Washakie," McLaughlin said.

"Now I would like to hear what you are going to offer me for my spring, then I will know what to do. That is all I have to say. I will listen to you." Washakie said, sitting down after speaking.

"I would now like to hear from Chief Sharp Nose, of the Arapahoes, after which I will make you an offer," McLaughlin said.

"My friend, we are glad to see you, and now that we see you here we are glad you are with us. You are the kind man we like to see. My friend, you have been with the Sioux twenty-four years, and you know all about the Indians. You know that they are poor. I think that the Great Father told you how much he is going to pay for this hot spring and I want you to tell me how much he is going to pay for this hot spring and I want you to tell me how much you are willing to give for it.

If you tell me how much this offer is, then you will hear after a while what we want. That is what we are all here for — about the spring. I will make this treaty good, and on that account I want you to pity me and not to cheat me at all. I want to fix this treaty straight. No lies about it. Now, that is all I have to say. I want to hear from you," Sharp Nose said, looking at McLaughlin.

"Washakie said he at one time lived at the hot springs, but as the game had disappeared from that section he moved away, and was not living here in the Wind River Valley. In selecting this location for a home he acted wisely, as this is a good section of the country. Sharp Nose says that his people are poor, and that he wishes this agreement made straight, without any lies in it. That is what I also wish. As I am the representative of the Great Father in this negotiation I do not wish any lies in it, and while I agree with Sharp Nose that these Indians are poor in a certain sense, yet they are rich in valuable land. I have visited, many other reservations, but I have found none that excels or even equals the land in Big Wind, Little Wind, and Popoagie valleys, but I recognize the fact that, in order that the Indians may be able to cultivate the land, they need some assistance, and I am prepared to make you an offer for that tract of 10 miles square of land, embracing the hot springs on Big Horn River; that will aid you to develop your farms, and make that industry more profitable than is possible with your present means. My instructions say that it is believed that $50,000 would be a fair offer for the spring and the tract of 10 miles square surrounding it, but after looking over the country and considering the needs of the people, I have concluded to add $10,000 more to that amount, making $60,000. The offer that I now make you is all that I believe Congress would ratify, and I feel quite certain that a greater amount would not be ratified," McLaughlin said.

(Washakie here talked to his people, saying that yesterday all day he tried to count $50,000 but he could not do it.)

I will now submit the following three propositions:

FIRST: The Indians to receive $10,000 a year for six years. To be expended as the Secretary of the Interior may deem best in the civilization, industrial education, and subsistence of the Indians. The subsistence to be of bacon, sugar, and coffee.

SECOND: The Indians to receive $10,000 a year, as proposed in first offer, for four years. The first two years to expend $10,000 each year for cattle, in addition to the subsistence, or if the Indians did not think they could care for their cattle the first two years, they could make take them the two succeeding years. (Illustrated with matches).

THIRD: The Indians to receive $10,000 a year, as in first offer for five years, in addition to which they will receive $10,000 in cash the first year. This offer is the same as the first, except that the payment for the sixth year is dropped and the amount paid in cash the first year in addition to the subsistence.

"I consider the second proposition the best, but your agent thinks the first one the better, and I always defer to and consider the agent's opinions on subjects of interest to his Indians, especially when the agent is such a just one as yours. To give you time to consider these propositions we will now adjourn until 4 o'clock," McLaughlin said.

"I would like to know when this money will be paid," Washakie said directly.

"The money will be paid as soon as possible after the agreement has been ratified by Congress. If the agreement is made now it might be gotten through Congress during the present session; if not, it would have to lay over until the following session, which meets next December," McLaughlin responded.

"I would like to have the money right away. I am getting old and may not live to enjoy it, unless it comes soon," Washakie added.

"I promise you that just as soon as I can get the papers through, I will forward them. Now, if there is anything you wish to see me about while you are conferring, let me know, and I will meet you with pleasure," McLaughlin said.

"I would like to see some of the money," Washakie said.

"The bacon, coffee, and sugar will do you more good," Captain Wilson said.

An argument erupted between the tribes over this last point.

Council adjourned at 1:30 p.m., and scheduled meet again at 4. When the reconvened Washakie was the first to speak.

"I would like each tribe to get $30,000 for these springs," Washakie said.

"I cannot negotiate with you for this tract as separate tribes, but as one, as you are known to the Great Father as one people. I came to negotiate with you as one people, and you must agree among yourselves on some one of the three propositions," McLaughlin said.

"I told you that I wish to keep one spring for myself and my soldiers, but will sell the other," Washakie said.

A controversy occurred between the two tribes after Washakie spoke.

"Now, you have plenty of time, and I want you to talk it over and settle-it among yourselves," Captain Wilson said to the Shoshone and Arapahoe assembled. After some time, they came back to council and said:

"All these, my people, agree about the $60,000

taking $10,000 a year in rations for five years and $10,000 additional in cattle the first year. Men are like horses - they cannot work without rations. My people can work and earn money, provided they have some assistance to begin with, and open up farms, and need food to assist them more than anything else. If they take money it won't last long, The Indians will go out and play cards and lose it all the first day. All my children are very poor, and they think they had better take cattle and rations. The Great Father sent you here to buy the springs from us. The Arapahoes don't like to take the cash, so now I say we will take the $60,000, $10,000 a year for five years in rations, and $20,000 the first year, ten in rations and ten in cattle," Sharp Nose said.

"I want to say now to both people, that what Sharp Nose has said is good, and they had better take that. I say this because I am a good friend to both tribes," Captain Wilson said avoiding eye contact.

"I wish to say that Sharp Nose's speech was good. It is practical and reasonable. Money would soon pass out of your hands, while the cattle would Increase in value every year. I would recommend 2-year-old heifers. They would be better than old cows; they do not cost so much, and are more profitable. There is now very little difference in what you two tribes desire, only the manner of payment. 'The Shoshones want cash, while the Arapahoes want cattle. Either way will be satisfactory to me, but you must agree upon how you want the amount paid," McLaughlin said.

"I am afraid it will be as it was in former times. The two tribes would fail to agree. I am poor, but do not care if I am," Wahsakie said.

"Now, you must agree among yourselves," said McLaughlin.

"I have been poor a good while and expect to continue so. I always thought as if the land belonged to me, but I think now that somebody always gets ahead of me. I was the first to come here, and I think I ought to be the first to get what I want," Washakie responded.

"You have asked me to sell the springs for you; now you have the opportunity, and you won't have it again within a year," Captain Wilson responded.

"I told you I wanted to sell the springs," said Washakie.

"Have you talked with Dick, Bishop, and others of the tribe?" Wilson asked.

"They have nothing to say. They let me do all the talking. I am chief and whatever I do the others all agree to. The other tribe has too many chiefs," Washakie said, casting his glance at Sharp Nose.

"All my friends are here. We are going to make this treaty all good. There is $60,000 in all. The first year $5,000 in cash to the Shoshones and $5,000 to the Arapahoes. Our cash to be paid to the agent, and he to buy cattle for the tribe with it. Ten thousand dollars in rations the first and the four following years," Sharp Nose said.

"The Shoshones want just the same. The money will be divided per capita among the 1,744 Indians, each one getting his pro rata share, Is that satisfactory?" McLaughlin said to a loud applause building.

If that meets with your approval I will have the paper ready for your signatures by tomorrow morning," said McLaughlin smiling and looking into the eyes of the tribesman.

"How much will each Indian get?" Washakie asked.

"Provided there are 1,744 persons, as shown by the last census, you will receive $5.73 apiece. A family of four persons will get $22.92," said Mc-Laughlin to louder applause than before.

Numerous Shoshones expressed their desire to take cattle, as the Arapahoes were to do.

'It will take me some time to get the agreement written out and ready for you to sign. You must remain here until you sign it. If you have not enough to eat, it will be furnished to you. It pleases me very much to see you all now understand each other," Mc-Laughlin said.

The council then adjourned until the following morning.

The council met at again at 11 o'clock, April 21, 1896, for the purpose of signing the agreement.

"I have asked Captain Loud, commanding the post of Fort Washakie, to read the agreement aloud to you and have it interpreted to you sentence by sentence, to the two tribes," McLaughlin said.

The articles of Agreement were read by Capt. John S. Loud, Ninth Cavalry, United States Army.

"These Indians want the freighting of Indian supplies to be given to them," George Terry added.

"I will recommend that the Indians be given the preference in all cases," Inspector McLaughlin said.

"I have given you the springs; my heart feels good," Washakie said, looking at the men around him.

"I am very glad to hear what you have to say, and whatever you do I like it. I wish a copy of this agreement, as I have never had one before. I want this right and straight. I never tell lies. I want to help the Great Father, and everything is done now. After this I want each man's rations weighed; no more scoops or shovels to be used. I always liked the Great Father, and wish to do what he wants. If he wants me to work I will do so. If I am working and need things, will the Great Father give them to me?" Sharp Nose asked.

"Yes; provided there is money left from the amount for subsistence, and I think there will be a few hundred dollars," McLaughlin said.

"I would also like a copy of the agreement," Washakie said.

"I will give you each a copy of the agreement," McLaughlin said.

"I would like to know if they are going to hurry the cars (railroad) in there where they bought the springs?" Washakie asked.

I cannot say; but believe that some of the railroad companies will very probably build a branch line in that direction, bringing a railroad point nearer than at present," McLaughlin said.

Washakie, chief of the Shoshones, signed the agreement at 12 o'clock p.m., saying, as he did so, "I never tell lies."

Sharp Nose, chief of the Arapahoes, signed next: then Bishop, who said the same as Washakie. Other Shoshones and Arapahoes followed until 273 had signed the agreement, which was completed at 4:30 p.m., when the council adjourned.*

The Secretary of the Interior finished reading the transcript before the men in Washington who were gathered there to better understand how the deal was made in Wyoming and what it would accomplish.

"Inspector McLaughlin," Vice President Adlai Ewing Stevenson called out. "I have looked into this deal a fair matter and I want to know from you what you think will become of this land if we are to purchase it. And better yet, what is to become of the two tribes that are at the center of this deal?"

"Thank you Mr. Vice President and I would like to thank you for the opportunity to be here before you to explain my perspective on this complex land and people. I had the opportunity to travel to the springs with Chief Sharp Nose and Chief Washakie's son Dick just over a month ago.

Frankly, I see two tribes trying to survive in a rapidly changing world they find themselves kept out of and worse yet, without land or identity. They want desperately to be able to fend for themselves and live a self-sustaining life on the reservation lands, farming and ranching as opposed to their nomadic lifestyle of the past. The plains are gone. The buffalo are gone and the spirit of the tribes is all but gone, dwindling by the day and week as they struggle to hang on, starving.

If we give them the chance here to start their farms and get going in a direction outside of starving, they have a chance to reclaim some of their freedom through the land that has now been given to them."

"That is all good and dandy, Sir, but how are we to go about this business of purchasing the land? I am told the purchase is to be done through increments of monies to be paid in $10,000 sums and goods for six years," Stevenson said. "Is that figure correct, Mr. McLaughlin?"

"That is the agreement that I have made with the honor I have earned through being truthful with the tribes. The respect they give me is only as good as the word I have given them. Chief Washakie is getting older and he would like to have some of the fruits of this sale to enjoy before he leaves this world. He asked me personally when the money for the agreement would be available and I told him it would be available as soon as the agreement was ratified," McLaughlin said in response.

"Can you tell us then, Inspector, about the journey you just described with Sharp Nose and Washakie's son?"

McLaughlin let out a big sigh and cleared his throat.

"I would be happy to do so Mr. Vice President, but I warn the tale is not short and it often shows the human side of both myself and of the men I had the opportunity to traverse these lands with. I was given the chance to see it through their eyes, and that experience is what I will tell to you now."

"Very well, Sir. The floor is yours," Stevenson said, taking a seat.

"In all of my times serving in the capacity that I have as an Indian agent for the federal government, I have come to learn that the most important tool in this business and in life often times, is to earn the trust of those you are working with. The trust these tribes had in me started from the minute I arrived in the Wind River lands.

The truth of the matter is the fate of the treaty and the hot springs, which are called the 'Smoking Waters' by the tribes, was decided long before we entered into negotiations with the tribes to purchase them. Washakie did not want to sell the springs as long as there was hunting to be had on the land and there was still game for him and his tribe to hunt. Once the game started to dry up and Washakie was pestered even more to sell the springs, he had already made up his mind that it was time to sell the springs. I had learned this information from Washakie's son, Dick before we even set out on the journey.

One thing that gave my efforts predetermined success was the fact that I spoke fluent Sioux, having learned it from my time with Sitting Bull and his people. I was also fluent in the universal language of Indian Sign. By having the ability to speak directly with the chiefs without the need of an interpreter made the job much easier. It put me on a level with the chiefs that I would never have been able to achieve had it not been for these practical skills that proved to be invaluable.

I arrived by rail in March of this year in the town of Rawlins and from there I was able to take a stage through thick mud and freezing spring storms. Despite all the country could throw at us, we made the 150-mile journey in three days. When we arrived at Fort Washakie, and after speaking with Captain Wilson at length and listening to the complaints of the natives at the fort, I decided to make the journey to the springs myself to see what conditions were present there.

I suggested the tribes form a committee of

three men each, chosen by the chiefs, to accompany me on the journey to the springs. I found quickly there was an innate difference between the Shoshone and Arapahoe. There was also a fundamental difference between the two tribes and the Sioux which I had previous experience with.

This was my first assignment as Indian Inspector Agent and it was conveyed to me this would be a difficult assignment on account of the discord that existed between the two tribes. It was apparent in the way they looked at each other and spoke to one another. There was no love lost between these two ancient enemies, that as fate would have it, cast them as neighbors in reservation life.

Chief Washakie of the Shoshone could not make the journey on account of his age and poor health, so he chose his son Dick, Mo-yo-vo, and Bishop and a translator to represent their proud tribe. As for Chief Sharp Nose and I, it was found that there was no interpreter needed to converse with the Arapahoe tribe. The chief's wife spoke fluent Sioux and that immediately gave an element of trust between Sharp Nose and myself as we could converse with the aid of his wife. Along with the chief of the Arapahoes and his wife, there were Tallow and Lone Bear chosen to make the journey.

Prior to setting out on the long journey to the springs from the fort, I was instructed to use caution in the route we were to take. The commander gave fair warning to myself and the others that he thought the easiest route would be north of the fort across the Owl Creek mountains. He instructed me that the Red Canyon route through the Mexican Pass was not safe and although shorter in distance, the commander advised we take the longer route north. This was in direct conflict with the advice Sharp Nose was giving, as he and his tribe wanted to take the more dangerous route.

After considering this for a few minutes, I knew it would be unwise to go against the advice of Sharp Nose. I kindly thanked the commander for his concern and advised him we would take the route the chief suggested.

I believe this was the start of how I earned the ear and trust of the Arapahoe in the matter of the springs. They had grown accustomed to not being listened to. The risk was minimal and the choice was an easy one," McLaughlin said, taking a moment to drink from the glass of cold water before him.

Stevenson grabbed the opportunity to impune an air of importance, saying, "Can you tell us then about the land itself and what it was like to travel with such companions to the springs themselves?"

McLaughlin thought for a moment, collecting his himself. "The land is wild and unrelenting. It is a hard country where the wind incessantly blows without mercy. The sagebrush and greasewood rule the bea soil, along with deer, antelope, elk, and moose. There are bears in the mountains nearby and as we traveled, the chiefs told me tales of long ago when the land was even more wild. They told me stories of how the two tribes were enemies and would fight each other often, killing other members of the tribe through the generations.

They found it strange they were now cast together to make this deal as one people when not that long ago they were fierce enemies.

Dick Washakie proved to be invaluable in the relations as well, having known him for some time now I was able to gain insight from him on how his father would handle the negotiations.

He was a quiet man, and I believe it was from the knowledge his people would never live as they had before. Dick Washakie held no illusions reservation life was the end of the old way and the transition of the new way where life would never be the same for his father's people.

It was through Dick I learned of the intentions of the Shoshone tribe. Chief Washakie spoke for the entirety of the Shoshone tribe while Chief Sharp Nose was one of many to speak for his tribe.

When Washakie spoke, the Shoshone listened and they did not question his unbridled authority. Dick expressed to me his father was finally willing to sell the land because he did not believe he had many years left to live. Dick also was the one who showed me the plight of his people long after the deal would be made.

He made me understand this land we were looking to purchase from them had always been sacred. To prohibit access after the sale of the land would close another part of their souls after losing so much already.

It was from the journey itself I came to see there is more to this life than money for some. There is more to a deal than a handshake and the exchange of money. It was the land itself holding us together and the waters were a gift to mankind that should be shared. It's the way it had always been with the waters. I thought of the ancient baths in Rome and wondered if these very springs could one day rival those of ancient times. The only thing that kept this and the great springs in Arkansas different was their location, I had been told.

We started out in the morning on April 8th. We were an unlikely party all traveling together for the single purpose of the springs. We headed east and after about 15 miles, we came to Wind River and we traversed it, stopping to eat at a farm owned by a half-Mexican man. After eating, we continued on through a pleasant rolling country that showed itself to us in the early spring. The country is unlike any I have seen in the neighboring territories and states. Sagebrush and greasewood dot the landscape along with deer, elk, moose, and bald eagles.

We stopped and made camp for the night at the Muddy Creek crossing. It was here that I was able to have a one-on-one conversation with Chief Sharp Nose in Sioux. I took his point of view in the matters of the negotiations. I wanted to know what it was that he thought of the sale and what he wanted to gain from it.

It came to my attention quickly they were concerned access to the springs would be taken from them like so many things had in the past. It was when I assured him that he and his people would have free access to the waters, as all people would have access to the waters, that he smiled and talked softly. He wanted my assurance that I would keep my word, as I was known to do so with the Shoshone.

As we began to talk of honor and trust, the chief revealed that he and I had met long ago.

"You gave our tribe food when we were starving on the trail to Standing Rock agency," he told me through his wife, who spoke fluent Sioux as I did. "You gave us something when you had no obligation to do so and for that, I remember you."

I assured the chief in Sioux that his grandchildren would be able to bathe in the same waters that his grandfathers had, that it would be the same, but different.

We understood each other and our points of view.

His wife was the one who asked me in Sioux the most poignant of questions. She may have been the smartest of us on that trail.

"Will you hold your word with our tribe and my husband and can you swear by the life of Sitting Bull that you will honor what you say here today?" she asked of me.

I told her, "I have held my word before when others have not. I cannot speak for any others, but my word here today will be honored."

She seemed pleased with this answer and was a true delight to have on the trail with us and was prone to singing in Sioux spontaneously.

And when we came down from the pass and Roundtop Mountain came into view, I saw the future of this place from far away and then it came into focus. Being that it was still early spring, the cold of the winter stubbornly held thick to the red soil, painting a white canvas anew in a spring storm passing through the land.

In the distance, what looked like plumes of smoke from a steamship dotted the banks of the river.

As we got closer to the river itself, many of the natural springs revealed themselves in the winter cold as they openly rebelled against nature. As we got closer to the big spring, we saw what looked like makeshift camps strewn about the banks of the Wind River.

"Those are where the travelers trespass on our land and bath freely in our sacred waters," Dick Washakie pointed out. "My father has allowed them to do it as he has left the evidence of these crimes against us for the Great Father to bear witness to. We have asked them to stop their trespass against our people, but they continue to do as they please. We have already lost much and do not wish to fight to lose anything more. We ask that if the sale does not go through that you see to these problems personally Mr. McLaughlin. We have known you to be a just man in the past and we ask that you deliver justice again in this unjust situation."

I acknowledged the very real problem they are having on the reservation at the moment and gave my word that I would attest to the situation to Washington and make you all aware of this very real problem that is being had by the Shoshone and Arapahoe.

A treaty like what we have been able to produce this spring gentleman is a direct answer to the problem of trespassers. The settlers there have been eager for a treaty for some time now and have already had the prospect of one treaty fall apart. The tribes are ready to sell and the land could be had for cheap in relation to their likely real value, but these tribes will need the funds this treaty generates in order to continue on in their evolution as farmers. Without this treaty, I believe there will be many a dead Shoshone and Arapahoe come late winter this year. They are close to being self-dependent in the way of farming, but they are in need of support on the journey there.

"They have already been given the reservation, McLaughlin. What else is it that they need to be given?" The Vice President said to him. "We cannot do it all for these people. They will have to make it on their own at some point."

"What they need is a standing chance to make it sir. They had everything taken from them and now it has been replaced by the reservation. That is akin to taking a baby from his mother's bosom and replacing her with a bottle."

"And what of the area we have made this treaty for, McLaughlin? What do you see will be done with the land itself?"

"We have made this treaty. Unlike preceding treaties, this treaty will be honored. It is time to follow through on the terms of the treaty. If we fail to follow through and get the funds for the treaty, then we have truly continued our history of bad business with the native peoples. This treaty is an opportunity to share the land for the greater healing of this nation and of all men. We have the chance to make something out of this rough land. It could be the destination of all pilgrims seeking better health if we just follow through and do our parts now. I have done my part in getting the two tribes to come to an agreement and now I call on the members of this congress to finish the job and give us a national treasure that is this place and always will be."

"That is all very well Mr. McLaughlin, but how are we to go about making the Congress honor your agreement? You were given an amount to negotiate with and you made an offer above that amount. Have we not given these people enough with the very reservation land we are now paying them for?" the Vice President opined.

"To that, Sir, I say there is never enough money we can give them for what has been done to them. We have the opportunity here to make the honorable decision as a nation. The choices we are making here will trickle down through the generations. We want to do right in this treaty and it will help guide the path we as a nation will continue to go down. Right now we are at a crossroads as a nation and a world. The Olympic games were just held as a worldwide competition. Right now, as we speak, Henry Ford is developing a machine that will give freedom to the user to go where they please. The past is behind us gentleman and I for one am thankful for that fact. We want to be on the right side of history here in our dealings. The very fate of our nation depends on it."

"You are right Mr. McLaughlin, the world is always changing. This country is moving in a new direction. There is talk of "manifest destiny" now," Stevenson said to the body. "With that will come a different direction of this nation and the world in the coming decades. We find ourselves at a precipice in our nation's history. They will look back at what has been done to that race and they will look at men like ourselves in this room as the perpetrator. We opposed imperialism and aligned ourselves with this sort of thought you now speak of Mr. McLaughlin. This is a complicated subject and if it were just purely for the land value, it sounds as if there is not much fertile land in that country in general, let alone in this remote section of it. Perhaps these sacred springs will one day become a national park like that of Yellowstone to the north which Grant designated in 1872. What have any of you to say on the subject in this distinguished body?"

The body of men looked around at each other before one spoke up.

"When Chief Washakie approached me as acting Indian agent at Fort Washakie and asked if I could write the Great Father in Washington about selling the springs to the government, I took to the task with great honor," Captain Wilson said, standing to be recognized. "It was with reluctance that he came to me and asked this of me, but he believed that it was time for his tribe to move on from the area on account of the game vanishing there. He, however, like many others, believed the springs should be available to the public forever. The Commissioner of Indian Affairs, Mr. David M. Browning, after receiving my letter, turned to Indian Agent McLaughlin for the job of securing a treaty between the two tribes. I do not believe he could have chosen a better man for the job. I have the unique privilege as acting Indian of the Shoshone reservation to say that the amount paid for the greatest hot springs on earth was abundantly low."

"The amount has been agreed upon for the ten square miles and the treaty has been signed by 273 male members of the two tribes, accounting for over 60 percent of the 457 men in both tribes," Stevenson said. "The time for negotiating has passed."

"I'm well aware of that fact, Mr. Stevenson, but I am simply stating these springs are indeed the finest in all the nation and possibly the world," Captain Wilson said. "If you consider the fact the sum paid to each of the 1,744 Indians is to be $5.75 an individual for this ten square miles of land, you will see my point clearer."

"Your point is one of the main reasons I felt it necessary to offer the tribe more than the great father gave me leave my dear fellows," McLaughlin added, raising his tone as to embody the seriousness of the situation. "These people will never recover what we have taken from them. There is nothing to replace the space of what we have left them, which is nothing greater than the worst space we have allotted ourselves. Their forefathers have bathed in these waters throughout the generations and wish to continue to do so. This is their sacred space. I ask the members of this body, is there anything you hold as something sacred? What would become of you if that was taken from you against your will with no chance of recovery?"

"We beg of you, sir, to explain yourself further," Stevenson said, holding the body of the chamber of men in his breath. "We here, respect your opinion on this matter. That is why you have been summoned here before this body to decide the fate of another race that is not of the same object of rule as we are here. We are in the position of taking lands none of us here on this day may ever see. We are depending on your experience, as we have all had prior knowledge of it. Your history as we write it today may not be the truth, and the truth is god's wisdom."

"I have held the scarlet letter that is the eternal badge of ordering the arrest of a simple Indian that defeated Custer on the ground that is now immortalized on every tavern's wall in the West," McLaughlin said to them. "There is nothing that I have not regretted about that day, every day of my life since. I often times think of how I could have willed another outcome, but that is my cross to bear for the rest of my days on this earth. I come to you from different circumstances than most in this room, and that is one of the reasons I felt akin to the native man and woman. Most of you will never come to understand the way of life for these men, women, and children who now live in foreign lands.

The land we are gathered here today to purchase from these tribes was allotted to them in a treaty that lumped two ancestral enemies together on the same plot of reservation land. This was an oversight that comes from misunderstanding and ignorance. We are here today because of that oversight. I have lived with these people and come to know their customs and ways. They have a different view of the world."

The men in the crowd began to grumble something fierce. They did not like what he had to say. McLaughlin remembered himself and all the things he had seen that they had not.

"We are inclined to ratify this agreement Mr. McLaughlin," Stevenson said. "But in order to do that we will have to get the approval of the congress and that will be no easy task seeing as you offered them more money than they were willing to give in the first place. You know how the wheels of the government move and they certainly do not move any faster when there is more money due than they are willing to give."

"The amount we have agreed to is nothing in comparison to the true worth of the land to the people. It holds a deep spiritual connection to them," McLaughlin said, remembering the wild rugged beauty of the land. "The springs would be a national monument, or park the whole world will get to cherish. There is no price for such a wonder. The health benefits and the ability to please the Shoshone and Arapahoe by allowing them to bathe in the waters create something truly unique for this nation for mere pennies on the dollar."

'We will do our best to get your agreement ratified," the Vice President said to McLaughlin. "From there it is up to destiny to see if your agreement will one day make a national park out of those waters. For now, we will mark the bill as special and get it through to the house. Mr. Frank Mondell, the young representative from Wyoming is eager to take up your cause with the legislative branches. It will be no easy task as the next session is coming up at the end of the year. It will likely take time to get the natives the money you have promised them. In the meantime, I would like to thank you for brokering such a deal. No matter how it turns out. You have done much for this country and those people. We are thankful for what you have done to serve our country. If there were more men like you running the show in the West, I dare say the entire situation would look very different."

The men in the room stood in applause as McLaughlin stood to address them one last time.

"Thank you Mr. Stevenson for those kind words, but I say that if we leave it at just words, our word to these people will never be valid again," he said. "We have a duty and an obligation to follow through on what we have promised. My reputation to these people is at stake and I will no longer be able to clean up the messes this government has made through broken treaties if this treaty is not upheld. We have the chance to rewrite history with this decision and regain a national character that is in jeopardy. We have a chance to right our wrongs through honesty and integrity if only to have the chance. We as a nation stand for things that are right, but we do not always do what is right. Our work on this matter is done. We have done all that we could do and it was no easy task. We will go from here on to other agreements where other tribes are facing similar situations. We ask that you treat these people as you would treat your own families.

One day we will look back on these times we occupied and see all that we have all lost and are the worse for it. And dear brothers, we have lost plenty. Ensure that the agreement is upheld here and we ask that you do it for the people who need this agreement to be honest and true. Their very existence depends on it."

Time heals all Things

McLaughlin went on to broker several more successful treaties after that fateful day in Washington. After the meeting, he went home to his wife, who was part Mdewakanton, and their seven children.

He told them all one night, while they gathered around their father and the fire on a cold night, that he had been offered the position of assistant commissioner of Indian affairs in January of 1895.

"I turned it down, you see dear family?" he said to them. "Because I had very strong opinions of how I believed the natives should be treated and I did not want my work with them to be in vain and ultimately overrode by a commission that did not understand them. President Cleveland then told me he wanted me to be rewarded for my work at the Standing Rock Agency and I informed him that I preferred field work. He appointed me the Indian inspector role to recognize the work I had done."

They were happy to have their father home and knew only of these things what he told them when he spoke of it on evenings such as this.

"Are you happy that the tribes sold the land the government had given to them, Father?" his youngest daughter asked of him.

"I am happy they came to an agreement and the waters are available to everyone for all of time, but I do worry that the deal will not be upheld," he said.

"Will you take us to the waters one day?" the daughter asked.

"I will take you to the waters one day, and then you will know why they are sacred to the natives. The water is said to heal even people who have gunshot wounds. Do you believe that?" he asked.

"If you say it is so, Father," she said to him.

Chief Washakie died on February 20th, 1900 at Fort Washakie, three years after the treaty was signed by the Shoshone and Arapahoe. The agreement on April 21, 1896, was the last the great Washakie ever put his mark on.

Chief Washakie was given a full military funeral, the only honor given to a Native American Chief in United States history. It was attended by Shoshone, Arapahoe, and U.S. soldiers that formed the largest funeral procession in Wyoming history at the time.

The monies the tribes were promised for the Big Horn Hot Springs and the ten square miles of land arrived only in the form of the initial payment of $10,000. The rest of the $50,000 promised by McLaughlin and the Great Father in yearly $10,000 installments was instead distributed in coffee, bacon, and beef. McLaughlin played no part in the distribution of goods associated with the agreement.

Black Sulfur Springs was one of the three active flows of sacred waters at the time of the treaty and was left to Washakie, his warriors, and his sons. It stopped flowing shortly after Chief Washakie's death in February of 1900. There is a monument to the chief where the Black Sulfur Springs once flowed at Hot Springs State Park.

McLaughlin passed away in Washington D.C., on July 28th, 1923 while still busily pursuing his life's work at the age of 81. He was buried near the Sioux reservation in McLaughlin, South Dakota. The town bears his name.

In 1910, McLaughlin published a book on his life spent with the Native Americans. He titled the book 'My Friend the Indian'.

On June 7, 1897, over a year after the agreement was signed by the Shoshone and the Arapahoe, and after much deliberation in the senate, the agreement was ratified and ownership of the land was promptly passed on from the federal government to the state of Wyoming after the senate could not agree to make the area a national park.

One square mile of the ten square miles was, "at and about the principal hot spring thereon contained, is hereby ceded, granted, relinquished, and conveyed unto the State of Wyoming," the amendment to the passed bill read.

The state of Wyoming had already passed a bill in February of 1897 accepting the land from the federal government in hopes the federal bill would indeed pass. Their wish came true and the state wasted no time in creating the Hot Springs State Park after the land was ceded to the state, where the waters became legally available to the public for free via the State Bath House. It is the only treaty of its kind the United States Government has upheld with the Native Americans to this day. At the writing of this book, the public is still allowed a free 20-minute soak in the State Bath House that is maintained and operated by the state of Wyoming.

The Wind River Reservation begins at the Wedding of the Waters and is still unnaturally wild beside the highway that runs through the center of the sacred canyon.

James McLaughlin

State Bath House 1912

Chief Washakie

Chief Sharp Nose

About the Author

Ryan Mitchel Collins is from Colorado and now calls Wyoming and Hawaii home. He is the proud father of two children and the husband to the best wife in the world.

When he is not writing, you can find him leading tours through the rain forest of Kauai, or taking photographs of wolves in the winter Yellowstone snow.

He has published four books — Everyone Dies Alone, For the Sake of Tomorrow, The Only Way Home, and The Gift of the Waters.

Powder River Publishing

www.powderriverpublishing.com

www.ingramcontent.com/pod-product-compliance
Lightning Source LLC
Chambersburg PA
CBHW070517200726
48293CB00007B/2579